THE ZONE

#9

BODY COUNT

Books by James Rouch

The Zone Series
#1: Hard Target
#2: Blind Fire
#3: Hunter Killer
#4: Sky Strike
#5: Overkill
#6: Plague Bomb
#7: Killing Ground
#8: Civilian Slaughter
#9: Body Count
#10: Death March

World War II Collection
#1: The War Machines
#2: Tiger
#3: Gateway to Hell

THE ZONE

#9

BODY COUNT

James Rouch

SPEAKING VOLUMES, LLC
NAPLES, FLORIDA
2013

THE ZONE
BODY COUNT #9

ISBN 978-1-61232-919-2

FOR MARK

Munich is a lively, vibrant city. Its people are lighthearted and carefree. If ever a city can be said to display a true joy of life, then this must surely be it.

Extract from a guide book issued by the Munich Office of Tourism, May 1989.

Munich is a city living on frayed nerves. If I thought it possible for a whole city to be on the verge of a hysteric nervous breakdown, then this is what it would be like.

Professor Adam Weiss, Head of Social Studies. Munich University. On the Third Anniversary of the creation of The Zone.

CHAPTER ONE

In the very center of the city, if you listened carefully, you could sometimes hear the noise of the distant battles. Major Revell didn't make the attempt. These were the last few hours of his seven-day furlough. He would be hearing the guns, from much closer, soon enough.

Outside the window the constant stream of pedestrians was undiminished, but most of the tables in the little restaurant were empty. He had only to make a slight gesture to attract the attention of the fat waitress. A moment later another bottle of liebfraumilch stood beside his plate.

The food was hardly touched. Revell pushed a cube of smoked pork with his fork, but could summon neither the appetite nor the enthusiasm to eat. He refilled his glass.

A distant rumble of heavy artillery fire intruded on his enjoyment of the first taste. Now he wished he'd chosen a place where the roar of traffic would drown such sounds. The planners could never have known that freeing much of the city center from the intrusion of vehicles would have brought that disadvantage.

An elderly woman, with two tired grandchildren in tow, came in and returned the waitress's greeting. She made to sit at the next table, saw the officer's uniform, and hesitated almost imperceptibly. Instead she chose to sit at another, further away.

Revell's smile at the little girl was rewarded with a shy but polite *Gutan Abend,* before she was pulled abruptly to her distant seat. He let the smile fade slowly. It was a reaction he was all too used to.

When he entered the small establishment, there had been a hurried whispered conversation between the waitress and the unseen proprietor in the kitchen. Revell had been shown to a corner table, far from the door.

Not that they could have refused to serve him. Even a few months earlier they might well have. The new laws had changed all that, if not the actual attitudes of the people.

Munich was close to the borders of the Zone, but divorced itself from the reality of that great contaminated no-man's-land as much as it could. As if it could pretend that it did not exist.

In the eyes of the civilian population—even those of the rear echelon staff who inhabited the city in seemingly vast numbers—combat soldiers carried the taint of the Zone with them.

The stories—mostly wild, but many all too true, of nuclear, chemical, and bacterial weapons—made the fighting troops outcasts in the society they were defending.

Idly he wondered if the wine was watered, but he knew it wasn't. At any other time the amount he had drunk would have put him under the table. Now it was having no apparent effect. His mind was too full of what awaited him in the days—and if he was lucky enough to live that long—in the weeks that lay ahead.

"May I join you, Herr Major?"

Revell hadn't notice the man enter. When he looked at him closely, he was hardly surprised. From his bland expression to his nondescript suit, the man was a walking nonentity. Out of habit, Revell tried to classify him. Perhaps he was the owner of a small and uninteresting business, or a bureaucrat in a minor state concern, the post office perhaps.

"Is there a special reason why you should wish to join me?"

"Let me introduce myself, however inadequately. My name is Otto. You do not know me."

Unbidden, he sat down across from the officer. Revell ob-

8

served that even his posture was unremarkable. Slightly round-shouldered, a little stooped, but not sufficiently to provoke comment. The man would have melted unnoticed into any crowd.

A dozen times in the last seven days, Revell had been battened on to by salesmen peddling everything from insurance to forged passports and replica medal ribbons. And there were others who approached men on leave. Usually they were relatives of refugees trapped in the Zone. They desperately clutched at any straw for information, interrogating with a pitiful intensity any soldier who spared them the time.

Somehow Revell knew this man was not any of those.

"Just Otto?"

"As I said, Herr Major Revell, you do not know me, and there is no reason why you should. Not now, not ever."

"You know me though."

"Indeed I do. I would have contacted you before, but the city is so full at this time. We lost track of you for several days."

"I can't say I'm sorry. I don't like being spied on."

"I am sure, Major Revell. Actually we traced you through a lady friend of yours, of whom we learnt only today, Fräulein Sophia Pruller. I'm sorry, I see you take offence. Please accept my apologies. That was an unwarranted intrusion into your private affairs."

"I think you had better come straight to the point." The German had Revell puzzled. Nothing in his voice or manner suggested any exceptional qualities, but he sensed that in him there were depths he did not care to explore.

"And so I shall Major."

Otto waved away the waitress, then had second thoughts, and ordered a mineral water. He waited until it had been served before going on.

"I represent certain interests, Major Revell. We have known of your Special Combat Company for some time. An

9

interest has been taken in you and your recent—shall we say—problems."

"Would you like to spell that out." Revell was not about to be tricked into revealing information, but he was intrigued.

"Certainly. If I mention a mass grave, and a KGB disciplinary battalion,* and your raid upon them? Need I go on to mention the charges you faced for disobeying orders not to retaliate during a truce?"

"So you seem to know as much as you say. Why your interest in me and my unit?"

Again there was an interruption, with the entrance of a large group of Swedish tourists. Two of the women were unsteady, and there was much chatter and giggling over seating arrangements before they settled to read the menu.

It was with surprise that Revell noticed his bottle was already half-empty. Perhaps the drink *was* getting to him.

"I have a proposition, Major. The men I represent are very rich, very powerful. They need protection. You would be paid very well."

"They operate in the Zone?"

"Some of their ventures are in that area, yes."

"And you want me to deliver my unit, complete, as a freelance army. You want us all to desert, in one go."

"You are a blunt man, Major Revell, but yes, that is what I am proposing. The men of whom I speak have urgent need of your services. They offer an initial cash payment of two million marks, for you to split as you see fit. That is purely a token of their good faith, there would be much more to follow."

"And when would they want us to go to work for them?"

"Right away, Major, right away. There is transport available to move you tonight. Your men are due to be assembled at the Hauptbahnhof at one o'clock tonight for the train at three, are they not?"

*ZONE 8. WAR CRIME.

10

Revell had heard that anything and everything was for sale in Munich. This was certainly proof of the truth of that rumor.

"So you think my men will go for it straight off, just like that."

"They will follow you, Major, I am certain of it. But you do not have to tell them tonight. We have the buses and the papers all ready. You have only to say that the arrangements have been altered, and that they will not be going by train. Later you can explain in full. Each of them will make many times what he does at present."

Knowing his manner and expression were being carefully watched, Revell did nothing to betray his thoughts. He kept quiet, waiting to see what else this Otto had to say.

"For years, Major, you have been fighting for a cause that most of your men barely comprehend. Let them at last reap the rewards that the risks they take should bring. Surely they deserve that at least?"

"I think you're underestimating my men, and overestimating my powers of persuasion." Managing to catch the waitress's eye, as she waited impatiently for the party's order, Revell called to her. *"Fräulein, zahlen bitte."*

He said nothing more until she had placed the bill on the table and he'd counted out the notes, waving the change away.

"Herr Otto, or whatever your name is, I don't think we have anything more to discuss. You've been wasting your time." Abruptly leaving the table, Revell went out.

The German waited a moment, then threw down a coin and followed.

Out in the crowded street, Revell checked the time by a clock above the town hall. There was no hurry. He would go back to the hotel and pack, then have a last leisurely shower. Sophia should already have left. He'd told her it was best that she was gone before he returned.

Their affair had developed at the same frantic pace that characterized all that went on in Munich. But right from the start, he'd made it abundantly clear that those seven days would be all that there was for them. She had fully understood that. You can't plan a future with someone who doesn't have one. He hadn't, not once he was back in the Zone.

There were no familiar faces in the crowd. Only a couple of times in the last week had he glimpsed any members of his unit. Ackerman he had seen deep in a conspiratorial conversation with an overweight staff-sergeant and two disreputable-looking Turks. That had been in a seedy cafe off of Leopoldstrasse.

Dooley had been strolling through the Hofgarten with the bosomy young girl he had met and fallen for up north. Then she had been with Fräu Lilly's travelling brothel. In the gardens she had been more demurely dressed, and the couple had been too absorbed in each other to notice anyone else.

It was hardly surprising that Revell had seen so little of the others. The city was packed with tourists for the Oktoberfest, due to start in the morning. He was not sorry to be leaving before then. The crowds would be suffocating.

The proximity of the war appeared to make no difference, though the hotel staff had told him that as the boundary of the Zone edged ever closer to the city, so attendance of the various festivals declined. This year, for the first time ever, there were still rooms to be had at most of the hotels.

But if sheer numbers were down, consumption of alcohol was not. Preparation for the beer festival had meant a non-stop convoy of brewers' trucks rolling into town all week.

Thinking of that reminded him of Andrea. He tried to imagine how she would have spent her seven days. Drunk almost certainly, but he couldn't picture her propping up a bar. She'd be a solitary drinker.

Perhaps he should have tried to stay with her. No, that

would have been pointless, and frustrating. Better to have met Sophia and enjoyed his brief freedom from danger and discomfort.

Irritated by the jostling late-night crowd, Revell turned into a side street, out of the press. It ran between anonymous glass-fronted office blocks.

The bellowing of drunks died away behind him, and he heard his own footsteps echo back from the reflective frontages. On each there seemed to be a softer, not quite synchronized doubled effect, as if his flickering shadow was just failing to keep pace with him.

If he was hearing things, then the wine definitely hadn't been watered. To clear his head, he looked up at the sky. The towers of glass swung back and forth overhead.

So he had drunk a skinful. What a pity that this was the first he knew of it, that he hadn't enjoyed the process more.

Dizziness made him stagger a half-step back. He pulled up abruptly as something hard and cold was shoved against the side of his neck, just below his ear.

CHAPTER TWO

"You should have accepted the offer, Major."

Steered by the pressing barrel of the pistol, Revell went slowly towards the darkened ramp leading to an underground service area. He prepared himself to turn as fast as he could, but suddenly the gun was no longer there.

"I think you were about to do something heroic, Major. For your abilities as a trained soldier, I have great respect. It would have been foolish of me to have remained too close. Even with a liter or two of wine inside you, I don't doubt your reactions would be much faster than mine."

"So what happens now?" Very slowly, Revell turned to face the German.

"I am not so foolish as to work alone either. My comrade is fetching our car. Ah, and here it comes. If you knew who was driving, I think you would be very surprised. This is such a sad world. There is so little loyalty."

A Mercedes station wagon cruised slowly down the narrow street, until the edge of its dipped beams caught them. It pulled over to the curb and stopped. An audible ticking from its engine revealed that the diesel had not yet warmed up.

"You want me to get inside?"

"Oh no, Major. The transport is only for me. By the time you are found, I shall be far away. To the police, you will be no more than yet another unfortunate mugging victim. All too common an event in Munich at this time, I fear."

The crack of the shot was whiplash sharp in the confines of the canyon of glass. A muzzle flash was reflected a thousand times in as many panes.

A scream replaced the report of the firing. At the roadside sprawled a figure, jackknifing and straightening alternately in stomach-clasping agony.

Revell saw the outline of the vehicle's driver moving towards him, an automatic levelled. At his feet, Otto continued to squirm and screech in a widening pool of blood.

"That came as great a shock to him as I am a surprise to you, Major. Is that not the case?" Andrea swept back her long dark hair with her free hand. Casually aiming the Colt, she put a single round into the head of the wounded German.

There came a babble of confused shouting from the far end of the street. Hesitantly, but gaining courage as numbers increased, a mob was spilling towards them.

"So stupid they would walk toward gunfire." Grabbing Revell, Andrea pulled him towards the car. "Do you want to stop and explain?"

Feeling as though he was being jerked out of a dream, Revell barely got the passenger door closed before the Mercedes was thrown through a controlled handbrake turn.

Facing back the way it had come, the station wagon fishtailed as it roared from the scene towards the open end of the street.

"What sort of double cross is going on?" A thousand questions raced in Revell's mind. "Were you with that character? Working with him?"

"While it suited me to let him think so, yes. Where are you staying?"

Revell told her. They had reached the junction with Briennerstrasse. Andrea braked hard to take the corner at a sensible speed that would not attract attention. Once out on the main road, she matched her driving style to the fast-moving streams of traffic.

"That murdering little creep offered me a couple of million to hand him the whole of the Special Combat Company

15

on a plate tonight."

At his feet, Revell noticed a case. He picked it up. The lock was broken. The bag was stuffed full of bundles of banknotes.

"Hell, he really meant it. When I wouldn't play ball with him, why didn't he simply go off and find another outfit? I can think of several up north that might well have taken him up on this sort of offer. And why try to bump me off? Didn't he like taking no for an answer?"

He looked at Andrea as she concentrated on her driving. Dressed casually but attractively in denim, no one could ever have told by looking at her that she had just killed, brutally and quite coldly.

Revell waited until they stopped for lights. "So what's your part in all this?"

"He recruited me shortly after we arrived in the city. Everything there was to know about me, he knew. I was interested, so I let him think that I could be bought and blackmailed, and went along to see what would happen."

"What happened was that you were damned near an accomplice to my murder."

"You were never in any danger." Andrea did not bother to look to see the officer's expression, but did allow herself a tight smile of amusement. "Although he was very professional, like most men he was also a chauvinist. He did not take the precautions with me that he would have taken with a man. I thought there would be a moment when he would be dangerous, so when an opportunity presented itself, I made sure his pistol would not function."

"Some professional. Are you trying to tell me that he didn't check his gun at any time tonight."

"Oh no. In fact his last act before going into the restaurant was to check the magazine and action. But there are other ways to insure a weapon will not function correctly. The chewing gum I pushed up the barrel would have set quite hard."

"Clever. He'd have blown away his face or his fingers, or both." The effects of the drink were wearing off rapidly, but a steady throbbing persisted behind Revell's left temple. He found it hard to believe that Andrea had dried out during the last week. But she certainly didn't show any signs of having been drinking.

Andrea leaned hard on the horn as a taxi cut in front. "So, have you thought about what he was, who he was working for?"

Though he'd been speculating on that to himself, none of the answers Revell had come up with were all that satisfactory. "Gangsters, I suppose, possibly a black market mob."

"Those were my thoughts, at first." Turning into the parking lot of the major's hotel, Andrea drove around the side before parking in an obscure corner. "But he had too much information. It is true that some of the bigger gangs in the Zone are very well-organized, especially those involved in smuggling out refugees, but they would not have bothered to find out so much."

"That leaves the possibility that he was working for the communists. A sleeper, a deep-cover agent?"

"Perhaps, or a freelance employed by them." Turning off the engine, Andrea settled lower in her seat and peered out at the wall over the rim of the steering wheel. "Certainly he was one or the other. I realized that when it became obvious that he knew as much about my life *before* I deserted from the East German border guard, as afterwards. More, in fact."

"Is that what sobered you up?" Revell was well aware that it would have taken exceptional circumstances to drag her away from the bottle. Discovering that her late masters knew her whereabouts might well have done it.

Andrea ignored the jibe. "If all along it was intended to be an assassination attempt, why all the elaborate trouble over so unimportant a target?"

"Thank you for that." Revell knew what she meant though. The city was crawling with senior officers who pop-

17

ulated the many service corp headquarters. You couldn't walk out of your front door without tripping over a general.

"Maybe bumping me off was an alternative plan. His main objective seemed to be getting the men out of the city as fast as possible. He and his bosses, or his controller, must have been upset when they lost me for those few days. Very likely they'd intended to contact me sooner, giving them longer to work on me. There would still have been the murder option, if they'd failed."

Andrea looked at the car clock. "It is very strange. In a few hours, we will be out of the city anyway. Why was it so urgent to get us away that little bit sooner. What do they have planned for tonight?"

CHAPTER THREE

He hadn't expected Andrea to accept the invitation to his room. While she sat on the bed and spread the bundles of notes, he took a shower. Out of habit he locked the door of the bathroom, and he was cautious when he unfastened it.

Hard jets sluiced hot water over his body, making him gasp. Everything had moved so fast. He'd let her take him from the scene of the killing without thinking about it, as if suffering from a paralysis of will.

How much had he drunk that day? The fact that he couldn't remember indicated that it was a hell of a lot. Certainly more than the couple of bottles at the restaurant. The hand he gripped the shower control with, he let drop, allowing the water to flow for a while longer.

Perhaps he should allow her the benefit of the doubt, and attribute their hurried departure from the street to sound judgement on her part.

The approaching mob, doubtless with many drunks, would quickly have worked itself in to an excitable state. Especially at the sight of a soldier standing over a dead civilian. Some among them would have rapidly convinced themselves that they'd seen what had happened. Their garbled and lurid accounts to the police would have made a spell in detention virtually inevitable for the pair of them.

Pulling on a robe, he went back into the bedroom. Andrea was looking out of the window. The broken case lay on top of a bedside table. All of the cash had been carelessly crammed back inside.

"How much is there?"

"I could not be bothered to count it. More than a million marks I am sure, perhaps two."

"Trusting sort our Otto, wasn't he, leaving it all with you." Revell began gathering his clothing.

"He told me the case was booby-trapped. I had seen him close it and did not think he told the truth. I was right."

Andrea turned and looked at Revell. "It is clear that you are not going to report the death. What do you have in mind for the money?"

His clothes bundled in his arms, Revell had intended to dress in the bathroom. Instead he dumped them on a chair, extracted his shorts from the pile, and pulled them on underneath his robe.

"I honestly hadn't given that a thought. Have you any suggestions?"

"Throw it away quickly. I have examined the notes. They are forgeries, and not even good ones. The federal German economy is in a poor way. If we are found with these, they will be harder on us than if we'd been convicted of Otto's murder."

It must have been the drink that was preventing Revell's body responding to the situation. But if the alcohol could block a physical reaction, it couldn't subdue his feelings. He was crossing the room towards Andrea when there was a knock at the door.

"Could we have been followed?" Revell looked at Andrea as she took a small automatic pistol from a pocket of her denim jacket.

"Impossible. I kept a careful watch behind us. There was nobody."

"The Mercedes?"

"I do not think we can ever be traced from that. Off the road, it will be at least a week before it is even noticed."

Covered by Andrea he opened the door. "Sophia!"

"I forgot my perfume. I thought if I left it until tomorrow, one of the staff might . . ."

She stopped when she saw Andrea, who was slow to pocket the pistol. Her reflex reaction was to look at the bed, and she saw the money.

Revell sensed she was about to go and pulled her firmly inside, closing the door behind her. "I'll get it for you. Where did you leave it? In the bathroom? I can't say I've seen it."

Andrea sprawled across the bed. "Perhaps she didn't forget it. Perhaps she only came back because she wanted to see you one last time."

"Try the top drawer of the dressing table." Sophia didn't take another step into the room.

Revell noticed a brittle edge to her voice, as he searched for the bottle. He had begun to think Andrea right, when he found the vial of White Linen that had rolled to the back.

"I'm sorry, Sophia, but this isn't what you think." It was hard for him to know what to say. He'd never been any good at handling these sorts of situations. Not that he'd ever had any quite like this.

"No, it is I who am sorry." Sophia looked directly at Andrea, who replied with a sardonic smile. "I jumped to the wrong conclusion. I am sure you are not paying her for any service. Apart from the fact that she'd never warrant the sort of price that money would suggest . . ."

There was a broadening of Andrea's smile, as she derived genuine amusement from the sarcasm. The stupid overdressed bitch, thinking that saying that would get to her . . .

". . . I've seen her sort before. There is no way she'd let a man put his cock between her legs, she'd prefer a . . ."

Anticipating Andrea's reaction, Revell managed to grab and restrain her before she could reach Sophia. The bottle of scent fell to the floor and spilled its contents across the carpet.

Looking down, Sophia spread the dampness through the pile with the toe of her expensive shoe. "There, it is in a good cause. If you cannot improve the company you keep,

21

at least the room will smell better."

With an effort of self-control, she went out, pulling the door closed slowly and quietly. Once outside the room, she realized she was shaking. She had wanted to hurt, to provoke the woman, but she had never expected so violent a response.

Sophia had never seen violence unleashed like that before. The eyes that had blazed above the snarling mouth had turned a hard but beautiful face into a projection of hate and fury. In it she had read an urge and passion to kill.

Still shaking, she took the elevator to the lobby and went to the powder room. It was empty. She put her head over a wash basin and was violently sick.

Andrea had calmed down immediately, wrenching herself from Revell's grasp a moment after the door had shut. She made no effort to follow. Instead she went over to the television and turned on an in-house movie.

For a while Revell hesitated to move away from the door. Gradually he felt able to relax his vigilance, and moved to the drinks refrigerator. "Can I get you something?"

He made the offer unthinkingly, as he withdrew a can of Holsten Pils. Finger in the ring-pull, he waited for her answer. She was lounging across the bed, legs trailing over the side. Was she going to stay off the drink? There was no way she could retain her place in the unit, if she continued to hit the bottle the way she had been doing until recently.

Not that she could be kept away from temptation for ever. This was as good a time as any to put her to the test.

"What are you hoping, that I will take a drink, give you an excuse to get rid of me? Perhaps though you don't. I think you want me to stay. You want the chance to find out if what that fancy tramp said is correct."

Looking past him, Andrea noted the contents of the shelves. "Such an interesting selection, but such silly little

22

bottles."

She looked up, and her eyes held his. Revell felt himself mesmerized by them. As carelessly as she had thrown the shot at the communist agent, she indicated a small pale green bottle.

"One of those. It is a snowball, I think. Shake it well, then come and sit by me."

As if his willpower had been sapped, drained from him, Revell complied with her instructions—her orders.

Stretching full length on the duvet, Andrea moved her fingers to the buckle of her belt and released it. Unfastening her slacks, she began to edge them lower on her hips.

"When you watched me touching myself, in the woods, you liked what you saw."

It was a statement, not a question. He nodded. No words would come.

"I knew you were watching. That was why I made it last so long. Now you must pay for the entertainment I provided."

An erection straining inside his shorts, Revell watched the gradual progress of her waistband as it began to reveal the details of her body. It felt as if each of her words was being stamped on the inside of his skull with a red-hot hammer.

"Give the bottle another shake. I want it to be nice and creamy and fizzy." With a last push that brought her head up from the pillow, Andrea's clothes were down to mid-thigh.

She sank back, closing her eyes as she ran her hands down between her legs. They lingered there, with the fingers moving gently. After a moment she withdrew them, then repeated the process.

"Open it carefully. Pour it over me. The bed does not matter. You are not sleeping here tonight. See where my fingers are." Her breath came in short gasps of anticipation. "Let it run just there . . ."

His face close enough to feel the heat rising from her body, Revell saw her fingertips tracing a path between the

23

tops of her thighs. He began to tilt the bottle. As the cream-colored foaming liquid began to pour, she grabbed his hair and began to force his face down.

"Lick it off. Drink it, all of it. No, not so fast — gently. Let me feel your tongue."

CHAPTER FOUR

The taste was still in his mouth. His lips and his face were still sticky with the cloying sweetness of the cocktail. And there was another taste that lingered.

Andrea's clothes were strewn across the floor. She'd discarded them as she went to the bathroom. He could hear the shower running. Through the partially open door, he could occasionally glimpse her, but he stayed in the bedroom.

While he waited for his turn to wash, he dimmed the lights, to look out on the city without their reflection on the glass.

Visibility was good, very good. A near-full moon was adding its cold glow to that of the city's more garish illuminations. Seeing it lit up like this, he felt instinctively nervous at the lack of any blackout precautions. Not that he had any reason to be, the western boundary of the Zone was still forty kilometers from the city center.

This part of southern West Germany had not seen the violent losses and gains of territory that had happened during the battles in the north. Here the Warpac forces were employing more cunning than brute force. Their advances were far less spectacular, often no more than a half-kilometer, but the pressure was as relentless.

Despite the Zone's steady encroachment on the city's dormitory suburbs, Munich flourished. Its industries churned out vast quantities of munitions and other war materials.

Sky-high wages attracted workers to its fiercely competitive labor market. Their salaries in turn drew in an army of civilian locusts to feed on them. Into the midst of all that had ventured several NATO military headquarters.

As word of the comforts and diversions of the city had spread, so more service corp HQ's had found reasons to move there. The pressure on office space had sent rents soaring, and land values with them.

Munich was a metropolis expanding to the very edge of a chasm. That chasm could swallow it effortlessly, as the Zone had already done to so many other cities.

As he took in the brightly lit streets and parks, Revell found his gaze being drawn further out, towards the east. Not from here, but from the top of the television tower in Olympic Park, he would have been able to see the distant band of darkness that was the Zone.

In all its thousands of square kilometers, the only light at night was that of tracer or explosion. To show a light was to throw death an open invitation.

"Not for us a quiet sector."

Deep in thought, Revell hadn't heard Andrea come in, her bare feet making no noise in the deep pile of the carpet. She came to stand before him.

The robe she wore was too big, the cuffs were turned back twice, and the material almost lapped her body.

"No, we've been promised action. The general will find it for us. You can be sure of that. Time's getting on; we'd better get moving."

"Why do we have to be at the station so early? We will have a two-hour wait for our train." Andrea reached for the cord to close the curtains, pausing to watch the traffic far below as it narrowly missed the herds of pedestrians constantly spilling over into the road.

Revell turned at the bathroom door. "Because I want to do a roll call as early as possible. That'll give me the best part of two hours to dig all the villains out from under the crap being piled on them by the provost marshal and

26

the civilian police."

He looked at Andrea. Despite the oversized garment, there was nothing waiflike about her, no girlish air of vulnerability. Damn her, damn her and her humiliating games. She'd only let him touch. Several times he'd tried to go further with her. Each time she had eluded his attempts. He should have got rough. Hell, even now he held back from grabbing her, and this perhaps the last chance.

"Are you ever going to let me fuck you?" Revell surprised himself with his sudden bluntness. He hadn't even realized he was about to say that.

Still looking out, Andrea took a long time answering. She watched his reflection in the glass. "Not tonight. Perhaps not ever. Do you think that makes your precious Sophia right?"

"I don't know." There was no anger, no passion, only resignation in his voice. He heard it himself. "I only know that I want you. That I . . ."

"No." Andrea shouted the word.

"No, don't say anything else. I don't want to hear any more, nothing." Hands over her ears, she pressed her face against the dark glass and closed her eyes tight.

Walking up behind her, Revell went to put his hand on her shoulder. It hovered over the white toweling of her robe, then he withdrew it. He felt he wanted to kiss her, hit her, make love to her and kill her, all at one and the same instant. It was that confused blur of emotion that prevented him from doing anything at all.

"I will wait downstairs."

Revell couldn't bring himself to stop her as she quickly dressed and went out. He couldn't even bring himself to say anything.

After she had gone, he stayed near the window. Some of the streets were looking darker now, as bars and restaurants closed. There was less traffic, and the crowds had thinned.

Across the rooftops it seemed to be getting brighter though. At least there was a glow. It was in the general direction of the Englischer Garten, the great swathe of parkland in the center of the city. He was about to dismiss it, turn away, when the glow adopted a flickering center.

Sliding back the glass door, he stepped through onto the balcony.

Yes, there was a definite flicker . . . and then confirming his suspicion, he clearly saw a tongue of red flame shoot above the rooftops.

"At least I'm not the only one who's had his night buggered up." Even as he spoke to himself, Revell observed another glow beginning to reveal itself. Though apparently a little further off, it was in the same general direction.

A coincidence most likely. There were a lot of crazy drunks in the city tonight. They were always at their worst, their most excessive, at chucking-out time.

From the street below came the raucous howls, screams, and shouts of such a group, adding weight to his theory.

Strangely though, he couldn't hear any fire engines as yet. They must have started up very rapidly. Still, a few pumps should have been audibly on the way by now.

The thought of Herr Otto passed through his mind, but he shunted it aside. There couldn't be any connection. That was just too fanciful. Hell, this crazy city was starting to get to him. Another week here, and he'd begin to be as jumpy as the civilian population.

Returning inside, he pulled the door shut, then closed the thick lined curtains. In the Zone, burying your head in the sand was a sure way of getting your backside shot off. Here, for a few more hours, he could still do it without taking that risk. Others were being paid to take care of Munich. It wasn't his worry.

Putting all thought of the fires right out of his mind, he hurried to join Andrea. He didn't see the third blaze start, or the fourth.

CHAPTER FIVE

"No, I have no idea what time I will be home. Please, Veronika, do not telephone again. We need all the lines. I am not shouting at you." Mayor Gebert took the receiver from his ear as the line went dead, then slammed it down.

"There are an army of pyromaniacs loose in the city, and she wants to know what time I shall be home for supper!" Gebert rounded on an assistant who was trying to lay a map over the litter of inkstands and ashtrays on the broad desk.

"You, stop fucking about with that and speak to that stupid cow on the switchboard. No, you cunt, not on the phone. *I* could have done that. Go and see her. Tell her that if I get — if anyone gets — a single personal call tonight, I shall see she is drafted to a women's battalion in the Zone."

"It is Fräu Pasch, Herr Mayor Gebert. She is over sixty, and not used to working the board when it is so busy. Normally on nights it is very quiet."

"I don't care if she's one-hundred-and-sixty. Spell it out to the old fool, and then get back here. Wait, if a Fräulien Ruth Stein should try to reach me, have that call put through to my private office. Otherwise only the civil and military authorities."

Gebert mopped his forehead with an already damp handkerchief. And to think, he had stayed late so as to enjoy a quiet half hour at the end of a hectic day. With the sixteen days of the Oktoberfest ahead of him, it was the last he was going to get for a while.

A secretary put her head round the door of the mayor's chambers and coughed discreetly to get his attention.

"Yes?"

"Herr Mayor, the chief of the fire service and the garrison commander are here . . ."

"Well, don't keep them waiting you stupid bitch, send them in." He threw his hands up in despair as the girl burst into tears.

The double doors swung open after her retreat, and two men entered. There could not have been a greater contrast in appearance between them.

Fire Chief Paul Friedmann was tall and surprisingly young for his seniority. His small sharp eyes seemed to miss nothing. In one hand he carried a walkie-talkie, in the other a neatly rolled map. He curtly nodded to the mayor.

Trailing behind him, in the uniform of a colonel of the West German infantry, came Adolf Klee. Pale, stooping, with eyes that made him look like he was half-asleep and was worried that the other half might join it, Klee gave the impression of a man who looked for things to worry about. His greeting was a limp handshake and an inaudible mumble.

Ignoring the colonel, Gebert tackled the fire chief first. "What's the position? I've only got garbled reports that make no sense."

Throwing the rolled map on the desk, Friedmann secured its turned-up corners with some of the cluttering ornaments. He tapped various locations with the stump aerial of his radio.

"I'm getting reports of fires here, here, here, and here in the city. Also several in the suburbs. Untermenzing, Fasangarten, the big industrial park to the southwest, the Olympic Stadium . . . See for yourself, I've marked them in black."

"Can you cope?" Standing back from the map, Gebert saw that with the exception of the fires around the Englischer Garten, the location of the outbreaks made a ring around the heart of Munich. There was no need for him to ask if it was deliberate.

"We're already on the scene at several. We should be able to bring some under control quite quickly. I have requested help from outlying forces, but they will take time to arrive. I've had to do that because we're so seriously under strength."

"The sabotage you reported this afternoon?" Gebert lifted a corner of the map to look for the file, but failed to find it.

"Yes, a lot of our pumps are off the road due to that. Mostly it's contaminated fuel, but we've also had punctures, slashed hoses, you name it."

"What's this I've heard about hoax calls?" Gebert had listened to the recital with growing unease.

As usual there was no change of expression from Friedmann's usual hawklike intensity, but a note almost of admiration crept into his voice. "Those are very clever, and we're getting a lot. It's making our work a lot more difficult."

"Have we caught any of those responsible for the sabotage, or the calls?" Colonel Klee had thought it time he had a say, as no one had spoken to him.

"The police are holding suspects. They've got nothing useful out of them so far." Gebert scrutinized the map once more. "And I don't expect they will. They appear to be low-grade sleepers, expendables who were given a task by a controller, who has since disappeared."

"Then what does it all mean?" Klee was confused by events. "I don't understand why you should need me here at this late hour. This is purely a matter for the civil authorities, surely. No military targets have been attacked, have they?"

For a moment Klee gained a little confidence as he made that point.

"Not that I know of. I'll check the current situation." Friedmann took his radio to the far end of the room.

"Really, I do think that this is a matter for the police." Klee shifted uneasily, yawned, looked at the time, and then yawned again.

"They're stretched to the limit already." Gebert made an effort, and managed to keep his language moderate. "In a few hours, the Oktoberfest commences. The city is bursting at the seams, and now they also have the traffic problems brought about by all the rubbernecks gawping at the fires."

Klee bridled up. "My men are trained soldiers, not traffic police. They have other duties to perform."

"Hell and shit," Gebert exploded. "Those garrison troops of yours are the worst parasites in the city! If it wasn't that they were sometimes called on to perform a few gentle ceremonial duties, we'd never get them off their fat backsides and out of the beer halls."

During the display of rage by the mayor, the colonel appeared visibly to shrink. He made a last effort.

"That is a slur on the men I command . . ."

"No actual military targets," Friedmann didn't apologize for interrupting, "but one blaze is threatening a clothing store holding army supplies, and another is half a block from a supply corp headquarters."

With a marker pen he indicated another four locations on the map.

"Four more fires in the outer suburbs. Might have been more, but the police have stumbled across a couple of groups in the act of setting more incendiary devices."

Gebert snatched up the telephone. "Get the police commissioner up here the moment he arrives . . . No, it's okay."

As the door opened to admit the man, Gebert had not recognized him for a moment. The police chief was not in uniform.

"My men have taken a few students in the act of starting fires. They made a run for it. We shot three. Two are dead, one in a bad way." Commissioner Stadler was listening to his personal radio even as he spoke. "He'll live most likely, and we'll be picking up the bill for months. The last one gave himself up, he almost shit himself. Singing like a bird he is, but he doesn't know anymore than the others we picked up for sabotage."

Stadler turned to the fire chief. "When will you have those fires out, how long?"

Freidmann busied himself over his map. "Several of the outer ones are coming under control already. Those in the center we'll let burn out. My men have orders to prevent their spread, that's all."

"What the hell good is that?" Waving his arms, Gebert stalked around the desk. "At the moment they've got a novelty attraction. When the crowds find out that the one they're watching is part of a rash of the damned things—started by commie agents—what the fuck do you think is going to happen?"

"Panic." Stadler knew the answer. "When that happens, we'll need troops on the streets."

"I don't think so." Colonel Klee was wringing his hands together slowly, sufficiently hard to make the knuckles go white. "If you really think it's advisable though, I could have a couple of platoons, or even a company, put on standby. At least that's the recommendation I'd make, if you'll back me."

"Are you afraid of upsetting someone? You worried about all the generals we've got in town?" Keeping his patience was proving difficult for Gebert.

"I command the garrison troops." For a moment, Colonel Klee felt able to assert his position, but the recollection of other considerations he had to be aware of swiftly robbed him of that transient dignity. "But as a courtesy, I will consult other senior officers, though I do not know if I should bother them at this late hour."

The mayor opened his mouth to reply, then changed his mind and ignored the man, turning instead to the fire chief.

"I'll tell the civil defence people to let you have all the dispatch riders they've got. Have them check out all the emergency calls, save your men from rushing about following up hoax calls. Anything else you need?"

"No, not that I can think of. We'll have things under con-

34

trol soon enough. There won't be many more fires . . ." Friedmann saw the look that Stadler gave him. "At least, I should imagine there won't be."

"I need those damned troops." Stadler didn't wait to be asked. "I need them tucked away up side streets, in platoon strength, in constant radio contact with my control room. I'll attach a couple of my men to each platoon, so that we can meet every legal requirement. I expect those pink shits from the civil rights crowd will have already been mobilized, so as to cause us as much hassle as possible."

The phone rang, and as Gebert answered it, there came a distant strident wailing that grew rapidly louder as sirens close at hand joined in.

"Thank you, Fräu Pasch, yes, I know. I can hear the klaxons for myself, thank you." Reaching down into a deep bottom drawer, Gebert rummaged about beneath piles of paper and extracted a steel helmet. "I think we should adjourn to the civil defence bunker in the basement now, gentlemen."

The calmness in his voice and manner was not matched by what Gebert felt inside. Seven times in the past year, the sirens had sounded. Five occasions had been for civil defence practice. Once had been due to faulty equipment. The other time had been triggered by a crippled Soviet bomber, still miraculously flying after being damaged and abandoned by its crew while over the Zone.

He felt that this was not an event like any of those. Already it was too late to do what instinct urged him to do. That was to walk to the window and take what might be a last look at the city.

Already switches were being thrown that would plunge the whole of Munich into darkness. Gebert made his own contribution, turning off the room lights. He was surprised at how bright it remained, with the moonlight streaming in through the big windows.

At least in the rush to the shelters, only drunks would be falling down and breaking bones. But there would be other

35

injuries, caused by fights to actually get places inside. The population protection program had been reasonably comprehensive, but the budget had fallen far short of allowing them to provide sufficient places for as many as were in the city at the moment.

As he followed the others to the stairs, a thought occurred to Gebert. Thorough though the blackout would be, and vigorously as it would be enforced by the police and air raid wardens, tonight it would not be complete.

Flaring in a circle about the city were those fires, and it the center, carefully spaced around the park, were the four big blazes the fire chief was allowing to burn themselves out. Munich had been marked out as a target, complete with bull's-eye.

CHAPTER SIX

"Stupid bloody way to die." Sgt. Hyde walked along the row of bodies. He counted fifty.

The last of the corpses had been pulled from the tangle at the bottom of the subway steps and laid out to await removal. Jackets and torn scraps of clothing covered the faces, but here and there a piece of material had slipped aside.

All those that the NCO saw wore the same terrified expression, eyes bulging, tongues protruding. The press, as the panicking mob had rushed the staircase, had crushed their chests and suffocated them. Many had died while still on their feet. Trapped and carried back and forth by the surging mass, their bodies had not even been able to fall.

"And not a single bomb dropped so far." Scully kicked a flattened beer can from the outstretched hand of a victim.

"Just as well." Burke redraped the exposed face of a pretty—or what had been—a pretty teenage girl. "Seeing as how we've had to stay above ground to deal with this lot."

"There was never likely to be any. Probably a radar operator with the jitters was spooked by a speck of dirt on his screen." Scully looked down the short flight of steps. "Amazing how they managed to bend those steel handrails. They even tore off some of the tiles towards the bottom."

"Think of it as a few tons of meat being shoved about." Corp. Carrington handed a purse he had found to a police officer. Many of the dead had been stripped almost naked. Every shred of evidence would be needed to assist in identification, especially with so many casual visitors in the city.

"Don't you have any feeling for the poor sods?" Burke

37

handed over a sheaf of identity cards he had picked up. Several were saturated with blood, or other substances he didn't like to dwell on.

"Don't jump down my throat. What I meant was, well, you've seen those westerns where stampeding cattle knock over chuck wagons. Same sort of principle applied here."

"People aren't cattle," Burke persisted stubbornly with his objection.

"I didn't say they were . . ."

"Right, back in the station you lot." Several times while his men had been carrying out their gruesome task, Hyde had been forced to step in and prevent bickering that threatened to be become more than that.

All of the men were on edge. Seven days among the fleshpots had been an attractive proposition at first, but Munich had been an unfortunate choice. Something of the brittle mood of the city had communicated itself to the troops.

It would not have been so bad if they could have gotten away quickly, but the major had insisted on their being mustered early so that the missing could be identified. And now the air raid, even though it had not materialized, was bound to create further delays.

From across the city came a brief burst of light machine-gun fire.

"Flak?" Garrett listened, but it wasn't repeated, though he thought he distinguished two or three single shots following it. "No, can't be. Too light, not enough of it."

"Shut up." Carrington thought he heard something. He strained to catch it again. "I must be imagining—"

A glass canopy above their heads shattered, and a body hurtled down amid shards of glass. It jerked to a stop a meter above the ground and swung violently back and forth, suspended from a tangle of fine lines caught in the roof's lattice girdering.

"Shit." Dooley scrambled to his feet, to be knocked flat a second time as the figure swung back and caught him again.

Blood spattered from the lacerated hands and face of the man, as he struggled feebly to release himself. A babble of incoherent Russian came from his gashed mouth.

"Paratrooper!" An instant after the shock, Hyde gauged the situation. "Scully, get up on top, cut him down. We'll want him alive."

The injured Russian was still trying, weakly, to free himself from his harness. His feeble, barely coordinated movements brought his hands into contact with the damaged AK47 slung across his chest.

Several closely spaced shots rang out. The impact of the bullets sent the paratrooper spinning like a crazy pendulum.

"What the fuck did you do that for?" Hyde rounded on the police officer who still held his Walther pistol. "We might have got something out of him. He's no bloody good now, is he?"

The officer looked down at the automatic, as if doubting it was he who had fired. Then he looked at the obviously very dead Russian and appeared to be about to throw up. He swallowed hard, his face staying drained of color.

"Im krieg totet man seinen Fiend."

"Sure, you kill your enemy in war, but we could have taken him prisoner. *Kriegsgefargen, verstehen Sie mich?* A prisoner of war, you understand?"

The body collapsed heavily to the ground as Scully finally managed to sever the tough strands of nylon rigging.

"You want me to get the chute as well?"

"Everything, and have a look for any equipment that might have got ripped away as he broke through." Hyde carried out a hasty check of the many pockets in the paratrooper's jumpsuit, by the light of a small torch. They were crammed with ammunition. His webbing carried extra magazine pouches and those too bulged.

A pack had been torn away and lay nearby. That the sergeant checked more gingerly. Its contents were a selection of demolition devices and .fragmentation grenades. Several

39

were fitted with what looked like booby-trap attachments, to give them a dual function.

Hyde indicated the ordnance to the police officer. "Dangerous, Gefahrlich. Put a guard on it."

"Looks like this creep sacrificed creature comforts in order to carry as much ammo as he could." Dooley had noticed that the Russian carried no rations, not even a water bottle. "Must have been planning to live off the land."

Audible quite clearly now were sporadic outbreaks of rifle and machine-gun fire, coming from the direction of the city center. They were punctuated by occasional grenade explosions.

"Pretty obvious this one wasn't on his own." Hyde looked up into the clear night sky. Only wisps of smoke were straying across the face of the moon. "The major is due back soon. We'll set up what defences we can right here, and wait for him. No point in us chasing off without knowing where we're going, or what we're likely to run into."

"Hope he's not too long." Dooley listened to the shooting. "I get the feeling all hell is about to break loose around here."

Ackerman was sore, in every sense of the word. His eye still stung. He was sure the blow from the MP's fist had blackened it. Shit, all those bribes he had been forced to shell out, and he'd still got busted just as the deal was going down.

The Turks had jumped from the back window of the warehouse. It was slight compensation to him that both had been prevented from making an escape by breaking legs on landing.

All that time and effort, and all those German marks, and for what? For a few short moments he had been on the verge of making a fortune. A couple of minutes longer, and the truck would have been loaded and away.

And now? The money was lost, the truck would be confiscated and the goods still sat in the government warehouse. The only ray of light had been the major turning up to spring him. Even then the provost marshal wasn't about to let him go until he had proof that the unit was going straight back into combat in the Zone.

"This ain't the way to the station, Major. Where we going?"

"I don't like to admit it, but I don't know. All I've been told is that the Special Combat Company is to place itself at the disposal of the civil administration. We're on our way to the city's command center, wherever that may be."

"Must be to do with the looters. I've been hearing a bit of gunfire. Must be more of them than the police can handle." The irony of the situation appealed to Ackerman.

The Audi turned the corner into Blumenstrasse, slowing to negotiate a partial roadblock caused by hastily abandoned vehicles. Their driver looked back over his shoulder.

"There was a lot of panic when the sirens went. There'll be more after the all-clear, when those owners come back for their cars. The local police chief is very hot on air raid precautions. Failing to leave the road clear for emergency services means that —"

The windshield shattered into a million interlocking fragments and became opaque. At the same instant the driver's head burst, smothering the interior and the other occupants with its contents.

At low speed, the Audi crunched the side of a parked panel van and came to a stop against an ornamental concrete tub planted with flowers. Its engine stalled.

Another shot rang out, and a bullet ploughed across the top of the roof to destroy the flashing blue lamp.

With the surviving MP, Ackerman and the major baled out and ran, crouched low, for the cover of a store's arcade entrance.

From there they could see a body in the road. Nearby a motorcycle lay on its side.

41

"Where's the fire coming from?"

Revell yanked the MP back, as he stuck his head out for a look around. "That's a good way of finding out. Where were we supposed to be going?"

"The civil defence bunker, under the New Town Hall. We can't get to it this way though. Not while that sniper's out there."

"Use your pistol on this door. We'll go through the building and use the back streets."

"Major, I can't do that. Damaging civilian property is a real no-no."

"Then walk out the front way. We'll follow, if you prove it's safe by staying alive for more than thirty seconds."

Reluctantly, shielding his face with his hand, the MP put a shot into the lock. His half-hearted push, to see if he'd succeeded in breaking it, achieved no result.

A full-blooded kick by Ackerman did better. An alarm clamored shrilly.

At the rear of the store, a locked fire door proved more resilient. It took a combined shoulder charge to burst it open.

With only the one pistol between the three of them, they could take no risks of running into any armed bands. They threaded their way through a succession of alleyways between the stalls in the Viktualienmarkt.

When they crossed an open space, a single shot passed between them, punching through the striped canvas screens enclosing a gift stand. There came a long clatter from within, as the shattered vases and figurines settled.

Revell realized that the shot could only have come from the tower of a nearby church. No looters would have hung about to take potshots. They were up against more than opportunist thieves. He struck off through a small plaza and into a maze of narrow passageways and courtyards.

"Who the hell is doing the firing?" Ackerman had picked up a short length of timber, in the absence of any other weapon.

Hugging the wall, the MP noticed with relief that the tower was masked by other buildings. "Must be commie fifth column. The police have been chasing after saboteurs all day. Seems a chunk of the local fire brigade have been put out of action. Kind of ties in with the fires in and around the city, I reckon."

Signalling a halt, Revell surveyed the route ahead. To get to their objective, they had to cross a broad avenue, Max-imilianstrasse. It looked the best part of a fifty-meter dash. There wasn't a shred of cover. They would be in full view of the sniper every step of the way.

CHAPTER SEVEN

They made the run in an irregularly spaced group, breaking from the cover of the side street and piling on all the speed they could. Last to reach the far side, Ackerman literally threw himself into the shadow of a wall.

No shots came. While they paused to catch their breath, Revell tried to make sense of the situation. There seemed to be small-arms fire breaking out in several quarters of the city.

Sabotage he could understand, but communist deep-cover agents were usually far more subtle than to start a mere handful of fires. War production and communications centers were their more usual targets, along with power generation, transmission, and transport. Burning down a few buildings was going to make virtually no difference to the NATO war effort.

If it was intended as a psychological blow, aimed at the civilian population, then strange targets had been selected. He'd seen a part of the growing list at the provost marshal's office.

Most were anonymous office blocks or unguarded warehouses. All they seemed to have in common was that they were individually and collectively of so little importance that they didn't warrant any guard or special security arrangements.

Munich was a vital manufacturing, administrative, and military center. And a cultural one as well. To Revell's mind, the destruction of any of fifty buildings that he could think of, would have had a more damaging strategic or morale effect than all these combined.

There was also the extra ingredient of the gunmen. The shots he heard were coming from several separate locations. Direct confrontation was a tactic enemy agents had never employed, except on the rare occasions when assassination attempts had gone wrong. It was difficult to see what a handful of them could achieve in a city this size.

The last part of their journey was down the narrow Altenhofstrasse, to the rear of the town hall. They were within sight of the entrance they wanted, when a bullet smacked into and ricocheted from a street sign post beside them.

It had come from the doorway. Revell had clearly seen the muzzle flash. He called out in English and in German. An answer came in the form of a burst of machine-gun fire.

"That's some of my outfit."

Starting forward at a lope, the MP made straight towards the opening, waving his arms and shouting. A second crackle of fire smashed his legs, and he went down screaming.

Again Revell tried to identify himself to the unseen sentry. This time he was told to advance with his hands up. Followed by a cautious Ackerman, he walked slowly forward. They passed the MP. His left leg had been virtually severed just below the knee. He was in pain too great to articulate, and watched them silently as they passed.

A few steps later, Revell reached the door and was allowed to squeeze his way in, past the heavy furniture being employed to partially barricade it.

"Oh Christ. Is he one of ours? Did I kill him?"

Revell took in the machine gunners pale, frightened face. "You shot one of your own corp, but he's not dead."

"Aw shit. Fuck it, Major. Why didn't you drag him in here?"

"You shot him, you fetch him. And don't leave it too long, he's bleeding heavily." Revell walked on into the building.

Ackerman grinned at the sentry. "Better do it fast, when you get round to it. You're not the only one taking pot-shots."

Another guard conducted them down steep stone steps that smelled of cement dust and copper piping. A corridor at the bottom led to a strongly constructed blast-door with yet another armed sentry.

This one was asleep standing up. Confused, he shook himself awake and pressed a signal bell. The massive slab of steel slid aside to reveal an airlock.

There was another pause, while the outer door closed and the air was sampled for contamination. Then the inner door, of less substantial construction, glided silently into its recess.

It opened to reveal a long, low-ceilinged corridor. Many rooms led off of it. Some they passed were open. Revell saw a telephone exchange, radio and telex equipment, a kitchen, and even a small gymnasium. Shower and rest rooms added to the impression that the facility had been fitted out very thoroughly.

Leaving Ackerman in the corridor, Revell was shown into a large room with map-lined walls. On shelves running below them were banks of telephones. Not too many of them were visible though. The room was filled with staff officers from a host of rear echelon units, all of them engaged in noisy debate.

A short, fat civilian broke from an arguing huddle around a table and greeted the major.

"I'm Franz Gebert, Mayor of Munich while it and I both still exist. Come with me, Major. It was only by luck we found you. Do you know, you're the only combat commander we can find in the whole city."

"That I can hardly believe." Making a quick estimate, Revell reckoned there had to be at least six generals and the same number of colonels in the room.

"Take my word for it. This lot might be great with battalions of packing cases and brigades of filing cabinets, but I don't think one of them has ever heard a shot fired in anger." Gebert mopped his face. He was perspiring even though the air-conditioning was working full blast, sending draughts of chill air through the complex.

"Did you have any difficulty getting here?"

"One rooftop sniper. Your own sentries shot one of our escort."

"Nerves, Major, nerves. When, *if* this mess can be sorted out, we may find we've killed greater numbers of each other than we have of the enemy."

Revell took an immediate liking to the little German, with his abrupt no-nonsense style. After the reception at the rear of the building, the sleeping air-lock sentry, and the confusion of the room, the mayor shone like a ray of hope.

"What sort of mess *do* you have? All I've been able to gather so far is that a few commie agents and sympathizers are on the rampage."

"It's worse than that. How much worse we're only just beginning to discover."

CHAPTER EIGHT

"There's someone I want you to meet." Gebert towed Revell across the room.

On the way they passed two generals in heated conversation.

". . . And there's a tank repair workshop at Furstenfeldbruck. Always a few sitting about on trailers, waiting to be shipped back to the front. A squadron of Leopards, that'll do the trick. Soon blast them out . . ."

". . . take too long, too much collateral damage. No, I say evacuate the city. Clear out all the civvies, then give the place a good drenching in Sarin, or any of the nerve gasses. That'll winkle out the snipers . . ."

The mayor looked at Revell to see if he had heard, and shook his head. "I've been listening to that sort of rubbish for the last hour. And those are bright ideas compared with some. This is Karl Stadler, our chief of police. He'll fill you in on the situation."

"The fires you probably know about." Stadler wasted no time with pleasantries. "There's a ring of them, right around the city center. Four here, much closer in, and two at either end of the English park."

"Significant?" Revell didn't need to look at a wall map to visualize the picture.

"We didn't realize so at first. The fire service resources were stretched. Compared with other outbreaks, these four were relatively unimportant. Also they were buildings that stood alone. No other property was immediately threatened. There were a lot of hoax calls early on, our

48

few pumps were dashing about to military headquarters, art galleries, gas stations, hospitals, high-priority stuff like that. So, I'd say that in those circumstances, a good case could be made for our fire chiefs' decision to let them burn themselves out."

"We'll be going into that at another time, Karl."

The mayor had been quick to see that line of discussion terminated. Revell could see why no representative of the fire service was in on the briefing.

"In any event, when the air-raid alert was sounded, the blackout drill went perfectly, but those damned things were still going strong."

"No Warpac aircraft homing on the city would have needed visible markers like those. Not with the sort of navigation equipment that they're fitted with."

"No," Stadler nodded in agreement. "No, aircraft wouldn't. They had to serve another purpose. We believe they were intended to mark a landing area."

"Paratroops, Major. Warpac paratroops . . . I'm sorry, Karl," Gebert apologized. "Do go on."

"The Soviets had a few bombers stooging about right on the western borders of the Zone. That was close enough to trigger our alert. After they'd kept it up for a while, they hit our radars with a spot of jamming. We soon got the measure of that, but while our screens were down they sent one of their big transports in on a fast sweep right over the city."

"No interception, no anti-aircraft fire?"

"None, Major. Surprise, plus some sabotage, plus the fact that our defenses have been absolutely stripped to the bone to bolster more active fronts are the main reasons, I imagine."

Still Revell found it hard to see what the enemy could gain by so limited an operation.

"How come, with all this in the pipeline, neither the

49

police nor the intelligence services got wind of what was cooking? Activating sleepers on this scale must have caused some ripples."

Stadler stuck his hands deep into his pockets and looked hard at the floor. "I regret to say that every week in Munich, we suffer at least twenty identifiable major acts of sabotage. Most are aimed at industrial production or the public utilities. Very likely twice that number are attempted but fail for various reasons. Also, there must be others that are so cleverly done that we can not be certain that we are not looking at genuine machinery breakdowns."

"We think there may be as many as one hundred and fifty communist agents active in the city. How many sleepers, deep-cover agents, there may be, we can only hazard a guess. Perhaps twice that number, as we are a university town." For butting in again, Gebert threw a mute look of apology at Stadler.

"But to get all this set up . . ." Revell persisted.

"After some earlier successes by my department, the Russians have adopted a new system for initiating and triggering these various acts." Stadler looked at the map, imagining what it would look like if a pin were inserted for each confirmed act of sabotage in the last two years. There was such a map in his office. He kept it locked from sight.

"Their agents get their tasks from a controller. Usually that's by a dead-letter box. There must be so many of them in the city as to almost parallel our own postal service. So, they pick up their instructions and make their preparations, construct a bomb or whatever it may be. The order to proceed with the operation they get by telephone. Sometimes they have as little as an hour's notice."

Revell could see the problem. "So, unless you pick up and successfully interrogate a suspect between the time he

50

gets the go-ahead and actually does the deed . . ."

"Precisely. Pick them up before they get the go-ahead, and all we find out is that something is going to happen, we can't find out *when* because they won't know themselves. We have little chance of discovering what is happening even in the near future."

"What about the controllers? Have you ever got your hands on one of them?"

"No, Major, but then, operating the way they do, they expose themselves to very little risk." Stadler ground coins in his pockets together. "I suspect that even if we *could* grab one of them, we would learn very little, if they in turn are activated in a similar way. What it boils down to is that, unless by a freak of chance we arrest a score of agents on their way to carry out an act of sabotage, we have no means of discovering in advance a mass effort like we've seen today."

"We have these basic facts, Major." Gebert checked them off on his chubby fingers. "Firstly, the Russians are prepared to put at risk an army of agents in this one operation. Two, they have dropped an unknown number of paratroops into the city . . ."

"An Antonov 22 transport might carry up to a couple of hundred paras. At least, that's a figure to work with."

"Thank you, Major. As I was saying. We have enemy paratroops in the city who, thirdly, have been able to disperse to unknown locations. That is in no small part due to the fact that virtually all of the population are in the shelters."

Stadler accepted a sheaf of messages. "My men are already reporting difficulties with some elements in those shelters. That is nothing though to the panic there would have been had Warpac troops dropped in full view of everyone." He flicked through the wad of paper. "My men are taking casualties. They cannot move in the open without coming under fire."

"What's the best estimate of the numbers in the shelters?" Revell was beginning to have an understanding of the enemies thinking.

Gebert considered. "I can tell you how many places there are. I was on the committee when the program was voted through. Half a million is the figure, if you include the subway platforms and the bomb-proof basements of hotels and office blocks."

"Tonight those numbers will be exceeded by a considerable margin." Stadler could see what Revell was driving at. "The number of tourists will have swollen that by perhaps twenty-five percent. Conditions will rapidly become most unpleasant."

"But at least they'll be safe down there, off the streets." Gebert knew he was missing a point. "What harm can they come to? Two hundred Russians cannot kill them all."

"They don't have to." Revell hoped he was figuring things wrong, but knew that he wasn't. "Let's work with that figure of two hundred. That could split into sections of about six men each. If we allow ourselves the luxury of hoping that a few went astray or broke their legs or backs, that leaves us with about thirty independent squads roaming at will."

"I was thinking they would stay together, or at most divide into two or three battle groups." Gebert exchanged glances with his police chief. "It could take days to clear the last of them out."

"That's what they're counting on." Behind Revell, two colonels were engaged in a shouting match. He had to speak up to be heard above them. "In the meantime, your good citizens and the visitors are bottled up with minimal facilities and severe overcrowding. I've seen their mood this last week. A lot of them are going to crack very quickly. If they stay down, they'll go mad, if they come up, they'll be picked off."

Gebert mopped his face. "You are right. Within forty-eight hours, Munich will no longer be a part of the NATO war effort. It will be a gigantic asylum."

CHAPTER NINE

Colonel Klee let the arguments swirl about him. Occasionally, when one of the generals would tug at his sleeve for attention, he would nod a pretence of agreement and understanding. His vacant gaze flicked from one to another of the faces about him. He failed to catch more than a few words from any sentence, and not a single idea from the hundreds with which he was bombarded.

Finally, dazed and bewildered, overwhelmed by the speed of events, Klee stuttered an excuse and hurried from the room. Outside in the corridor, he leant back against the wall, gulped air, and loosened his tie.

From inside he could hear voices raised, as the heated discussions continued without his being missed. He was fast persuading himself he was not well.

It was his wife and that damned brother of hers in the appointments office who had got him his present position. And why had he let himself be transferred from a similar post at Saarbrucken on the French border? Because she liked the stores in Munich!

Well, he had done all he could. At the general's insistence, he had fired off urgent requests for help. That, at least, he could be confident was the correct course of action. From now on the staff officers could formulate all the plans. He no longer had to accept any responsibility or blame for events.

Even as his churning stomach began to settle, Colonel Klee experienced a sudden feeling of utter despair, as he saw the police commissioner and Mayor Gebert bearing down on him.

Stadler was waving a message pad. "Are you mad, Klee? Have you really sent this?"

Klee accepted the pad, and put on his gold-rimmed spectacles to read. Not that he really needed to, poor though his eyesight was, he recognised his own handwriting.

"Yes, fifteen minutes ago. What else was I to do? They outrank me!"

"You have no comprehension of what you've done, have you?" Gebert's hands clenched and unclenched. It was only with an effort that he prevented himself from committing an act of violence on the elderly officer: "As a result of those damned cries for help of yours, we are shortly going to be playing host to contingents from every gung-ho outfit in NATO."

"The situation is worse than we can handle. I don't see that there is any other way . . ."

"So you send an SOS, an open invitation. When the Marines and the SAS and the Rangers arrive, how do we coordinate them, integrate them with your troops, the police . . ."

"I don't know. Let the generals sort it out."

Klee's petulant response to the questions was almost a wail of anguish.

"What more do you expect me to do? I didn't ask for this, I should have retired last year."

"It's too late for any of us to wish that had happened." Stadler couldn't feel any pity for the broken man. He had put too many lives at risk. "We have to avoid a free-for-all in the streets. How many troops have you got in barracks?"

Sobbing, Klee shook his head. Both his hands came up to his face just a fraction too late to prevent Stadler's fist connecting with his mouth.

The police chief made ready to launch another blow. "I asked how many."

"Perhaps three hundred or so, I think." Klee made no effort to staunch the flow of blood from his split lip. "We are under strength, and some are on leave or away on courses. I didn't know this was going to happen."

"What the devil is going on out here?"

As Stadler began to drag Klee away, a balding staff officer stuck his head out of the door abruptly.

Gebert turned on his politician's smile. "The colonel appears to be suffering from acute claustrophobia. For the sake of morale down here, we thought it best to subdue him quickly."

"Quite right. Can't have men cracking up. Especially officers, sets a bad example. Taking him to the sick bay, are you?" Not waiting for an answer the officer withdrew, and the door closed behind him.

As he disappeared, Gebert heard more snatches of the continuing debate.

". . . take at least three weeks . . ."

"need a couple of divisions I should say . . ."

". . . street fighting, nasty business . . ."

". . . a couple of mininukes will flush them out. Worth a few of our own and a chunk of the city . . ."

"We're keeping the whole operation under civilian control, using the police radio net." Stadler tapped the wall map with his marker pen, leaving an unintentional cluster of smudged red dots on the plastic cover.

"Most of the land lines are out, with the exception of the duplicated hardened cables to the airport and the barracks. If the damage to the telephone system is going to continue to escalate, then we could still lose them. So we'll rely exclusively on radio."

56

"A pity the trunk lines weren't knocked out before the colonel had *his* calls put through." Gebert glared at Klee, who sat slumped on a folding chair in a corner, taking no part in the discussion.

"If we stick to the plan I've sketched out, then hopefully we establish contact with the special forces as they arrive, and then absorb and employ them. Everything depends on this central control knowing the positive location of our hunting units at any moment. Most important, none of them must make a move without having it cleared first."

"You're expecting a lot of men who are not used to working like that." Revell was thinking of the hastily formed police SWAT teams that would shortly be going into action against the paratroops.

"I know. I'm spelling it out to them that with two columns pushing into the center, and with hunting groups already at work there, we've the ingredients for more than a few home-goals. Lose control, and it'll be a disaster."

That was one hell of an understatement, Revell knew. The first stage of the operation would soon be underway. Civil defence teams were making ready to lead to safety the masses who had taken shelter in the subway stations.

It was a daunting task, fraught with difficulties. The only factor that made even its contemplation feasible was that with each team there would be U-bahn maintenance staff.

Stage two was far more risky and complex. From the north the garrison troops, and from the east a mixed force of armed police and airport security staff, would have to push steadily in towards the city. As they came, they would have to evacuate every shelter and send the civilians back along the route they had, hopefully, cleared of snipers.

The columns would radio when they encountered serious opposition. Where they couldn't go around, attack

57

teams would endeavor to eliminate the obstructing paratroops by direct assault.

Both columns would be able to deploy some light armor, in the form of armored cars and personnel carriers. Their heavy machine guns and cannon would be invaluable for scouting and close support.

If the Russian paratroops had antiarmor capability though, the usefulness of armored vehicles in street fighting would be severely limited. With thousands of hiding places for ambush teams in every street, a rocket-propelled grenade into their vulnerable side armor would turn them into fiery death traps.

CHAPTER TEN

"You manage to get in touch with your men, Major?" Stadler groped in the pockets of the jacket draped over the back of his chair. He fished out cigarettes and a lighter.

"I'll be rejoining them shortly." Revell slipped on a flak vest Ackerman had found for him. "And I'll be glad to. There are too many high-powered staff officers here for my liking."

"Mine as well." Stadler lifted his eyes to the ceiling in pained resignation. "The generals didn't like being told that the operation was staying strictly under civilian control. A few of them I thought I might be forced to lock up out of harm's way. It is possible I still might. I feel they are plotting."

"Have you been able to contact the main police communications room yet?" Revell was aware that during their conversation Stadler had been half-listening to the operator who was trying line after line and channel after channel.

"No, I am afraid the headquarters will have been an early target. At this time of night, there will have been only forty staff members on duty. But we can carry on from here for the moment."

"What about the men who were actually on the streets?"

Stadler toyed with the lighter, flicking it to produce a tall flame. "I can reach about half of those who were on duty. When the sirens sounded, they would have stayed above ground. They would have been easy targets for the Russians, alone on the streets."

"They might just be pinned down. They're not necessarily casualties."

"Foot patrols and car crews all have radios. If they were able to, they would use them." Keeping the flame turned up, Stadler watched it absently. When finally it died to nothing, he pocketed it without lighting his cigarette.

"It is the manpower situation that is most worrying. After forming SWAT teams, those officers I have left are being spread far too thinly. Some are on standby to attach themselves to the columns as they approach. I have to dispatch most of them to man roadblocks as far out from the center as I can. As the morning goes on, a torrent of vehicles will converge on the city. Not all will be aware of what is happening."

It took little imagination on Revell's part to realize what would happen if a bus load of tourists suddenly appeared on the streets. "Do you have reports of many civilian casualties so far?"

"Too many. There's been no bombing, but no all-clear either. They've started sticking their heads out to see what's going on, and getting them shot off."

"At least it's not all one-sided. One of your men got lucky." Revell had seen the report. A lone police officer had come upon a Russian squad preoccupied with breaking into a building. He'd killed three before being wounded himself.

"I'd like to think it was more than luck."

"Perhaps it was. Either way, let's hope it's a good omen." Revell patted his flak jacket. "Normally I'd put most of my faith in this, but I think in our situation we'd be unwise to turn down any offer of help, even from the supernatural."

A messenger handed Stadler a sheaf of photocopies. "Here are your maps, Major. You'll see that the area I've allotted your company comprises most of the actual city center. By now they should be armed, I believe."

"To what extent I don't know. We were due to reequip when we went back into action. All they'll have is what they've been able to scrounge off the transport police."

"Then your first target will have to be the armory at police headquarters. Internally it's like a fortress after the most recent alterations. I wish you luck. Even with the assistance of a team of my men, it is going to be difficult to get inside, if the Russians are determined to hold it."

"They got in . . ."

"They had the advantage of surprise."

". . . so I'm sure we can. But I shan't be needing your help. I know the layout. We'll tackle it on our own, radio in when it's okay for your men to reoccupy."

Revell was glad to be getting out of the bunker. The chill in the air from the overworked air-conditioning seemed strangely at variance with the perpetual smells of cigarette smoke and lukewarm coffee.

It was a miracle it had not been an early objective for the Russian assault. Perhaps the section detailed to take it had been one of those to go astray, or maybe they just hadn't gotten to it yet.

As far as Revell was aware though, there was only the single entrance to the building. That could be defended indefinitely by a handful of men. The staircase and double-blast doors also made formidable fall-back positions.

Or perhaps they had never intended to try and take it. With the exception of the police HQ, they seemed to have gone for far easier objectives, civilian ones for the most part. Their principle intention appeared to be to cause the maximum disruption to the population as a whole.

"One last thing, Commissioner." A thought struck Revell. "Is there no word from the radio or television stations yet?"

61

Gebert had just entered. He heard the question, and exchanged glances with Stadler before taking the answer on himself.

"All local transmitters went off the air as soon as the alert was sounded. Also all relays of the national stations and cable TV networks. They make easy targets for emission-homing warheads."

"Good job satellite TV ceased when the war started. You'd have had a difficult task pulling the plug on them." Revell knew there was truth in what Gebert said, but felt he wasn't getting the whole story.

"Major, I won't try and fool you. It's federal policy that events such as we have here are given careful consideration before the media are allowed to broadcast a word." Gebert was trying to make what he said sound convincing. He doubted that he was succeeding. "Look, if we put out any version of what is happening—even watered-down—it's not going to put everyone's mind at rest, is it? What do we say? 'Sorry, folks. We've got a few red hit squads roaming about. Normal service will be resumed as soon as possible.' And it'd be picked up by other networks who are still on the air, over which we've got no control. Switzerland, France, Italy. They'd have a field day with it. We wouldn't have just one city in trouble, the whole country could panic."

"You know that down in those shelters, more Russian agents will be earning their bonus by sowing rumors, starting all sorts of stories."

"I know that, Major." Gebert offered Stadler a light, but it was waved away. "We'll have to rely on the police keeping control, or at least doing their best. We're having to accept the lesser of two evils. Better a few should have breakdowns in our shelters, than that a whole country should be made to run scared."

Stadler finally crumpled his cigarette and threw it away.

62

"We are going after these Russians hard and fast. No finesse, just straight at them hard every time we see them. Anything goes, a gloves-off operation. When it's over, there will be time for considered statements, careful press releases, but you know something, I'm dreading that time as much as I hate what's happening now. When the fighting is over, the witch hunt will start, for the communist agents who came out of the woodwork and helped create this mess."

Gebert nodded in agreement. "In the long term, Major Revell, it will be difficult to decide which has done the most damage."

CHAPTER ELEVEN

An ambulance had collided with a parked car. Both were burning fiercely at the corner of the main shopping street. Close by stood a fire tender. Among the flattened snakes of its hoses sprawled several of its crew.

Revell and Ackerman took to a side road that skirted the scene, using every shred of cover offered by doorways and street furniture until they were well clear.

The moon had set, and where no alleyway funnelled the reflected glare of the blaze, their way led through near-pitch darkness.

Distantly there came the intermittent sound of light gunfire. Once a single shot from closer at hand was followed by a scream of pain that choked away to silence.

Keeping to the darkest route, they passed through an archway of the medieval Karlstor Gate. They passed an entrance to the Stachus underground shopping center. At the top of the escalator, several bodies lay scattered. Loud cries and moans from below gave evidence that there had been other victims of the sniper's accurate fire. A figure lolled restlessly on the pavement, in pain too great to articulate. There was nothing they could do, except prevent themselves falling prey to the same marksman.

Beyond that there was another broad avenue to cross, but several strings of streetcars offered them a sanctuary halfway. They ran and dived into an open trailer car, throwing themselves full-length on the littered floor. Bullets punched holes through the panelwork and seats.

"Soon as we move, Major, they've got us for sure." A

round had buried itself in the timber planking immediately in front of Ackerman's nose. "They're firing down from one of these buildings. When we leave this crate, we'll be right in their sights."

"Just be ready to run when I say." Revell clipped the radio back on his belt, and waited. There were no more shots; he hadn't expected any yet. There was no point in their sniper wasting ammunition raking the trailer. He would have a clear field of fire soon enough.

A storm of tracers burst with a frenzied clatter from the far side of the avenue and flashed across its broad width. The noise of the many impacts on walls and downspouts blended with the shattering ring of breaking glass.

"Move."

Ackerman didn't need the officer's urging. Scrambling to his feet, he was on Revell's heels as they jumped from the streetcar, and a pace ahead by the time they reached the sanctuary of the far buildings.

The instant they hurled themselves into concealment, the covering fire abruptly ceased.

"We were waiting a few yards further down. I figured you'd be here soon!" Sergeant Hyde hefted the machine gun onto his shoulder. A half-belt dangled from it. "The buggers are firing straight down the Schutzenstrasse, and the Palace of Justice route is too open. Didn't think you'd chance that."

"Is this your first brush with them?" Revell had to jog to keep up with the men of the covering group as they made their way back to the station.

"We had one drop right in on top of us, and we traded a few rounds not long ago with a group trying to use Bayerstrasse. That's all so far." Hyde called for a slowing of the pace as they prepared to cross the last road. "I think we winged at least a couple, but their mates dragged them off, back into the center."

"Might have been better if they'd got through. Our task

is to root out and destroy any of them between here and the river."

"The whole of the city center? That's the best part of a couple of hundred blocks. How are we supposed to do that with only one under strength and a lightly armed company?"

"I know it's crazy." They'd regained the station fore-court, and Revell made a swift appraisal of such defenses as had been erected. The positions his men had taken were good, but Hyde's machine gun was the only weapon heavier than a machine pistol or pumpgun. "But if our mission is nuts, it's only a shade more lunatic than the enemy's tactics. They've dumped maybe a couple of com-panies on the city. I don't know what their commanders told them, but effectively they're on a suicide mission."

"Maybe they'll realize that for themselves and give up."

"I doubt it, Sergeant." Revell had good reason to doubt such an outcome. He knew a great deal about communist indoctrination methods. They were thorough, and in the majority of cases highly successful. "Whatever line those Warpac paras have been fed, you can be sure they'll be-lieve it. And they'll go on believing it until they're finally cornered and killed."

"So where do we start?" Resting the machine gun on the ground, Hyde looked out at the seemingly endless roads that radiated away from the railway station. Only one displayed any light, burning vehicles in the far dis-tance. Clearing them was more than a daunting prospect, it was terrifying. Using every last man, they amounted to no more than three-platoon strength. Such a small force would have been stretched to take a defended village, let alone a couple of square kilometers of heavily built-up city.

"We need the weapons in the main police armory. That has to be our first target. What weapons can we muster?"

Hyde was all too well acquainted with their meager resources. "The MG with three-and-a-half belts, fifteen machine pistols with three magazines each, and ten pump guns with a hundred cartridges between them."

"Couldn't you get anything more out of the transport police?" Revell had been hoping there were more weapons available than those he had seen being carried by the sentries and the section that had provided covering fire.

"This is all they had; they couldn't give them away fast enough. Mostly they're old boys with no stomach for a fight. Can't say I blame them. Bit different tackling Warpac paras instead of soccer hooligans. They're shitting themselves. Oh, there was a stack of riot guns. Unlimited baton and CS rounds for those, and plenty of masks."

"Get them, and all the gas grenades the men can carry." It was little enough Revell knew, but with it they would have to do the job. In the Zone they had often had to raid enemy dumps for ammunition and fuel. He hadn't expected to be doing something similar during the last hours of his leave.

Hyde shouted orders, then turned back to the Major. "Did you want to see the remains of that para?"

"Yes, while we're waiting." Revell followed the NCO to the booking hall.

Spread-eagled on the floor, the dead man's outstretched limbs and the dried rivulets of blood that radiated from him gave an absurdly picturesque sun-ray effect to the gruesome scene.

"Find anything on him?" Revell began going through the jumpsuit's many pouches and pockets.

"No papers of any sort. He had a satchel full of explosives, mostly booby-trap ingredients. Otherwise his equipment was pretty near standard, apart from the silencer for his pistol and sufficient ammunition to start a war of his own."

His search complete, and apparently confirming the sergeant's findings, Revell began to wipe the blood from his fingers, when for some reason his attention was attracted to the man's helmet.

The strap had been almost severed during his fall, and a hard tug parted it completely. Revell ran his fingers over its greasy interior padding. The hunch paid off, and he pulled out two neatly folded squares of flimsy paper.

Both sides of the sheet were covered with indecipherable Cyrillic scrawl. The smattering of spoken Russian he could understand was of no use to Revell.

"Where's Boris?"

"I am here, Major. Are we going now, please. I am told that everyone in the city is to be evacuated through the subway. Shouldn't we start moving?"

"What do these say?" Ignoring the Russian's hopefully phrased question, Revell thrust the papers at him.

Squinting in the poor light provided by a shaded flashlight, Boris put on his glasses and skimmed the text.

"There is nothing of importance, Major. It is trivia, an unfinished letter to a girl."

"I'll make the judgments. What does it say?"

"Of course, Major, right away." Turning back to the top of the first sheet, Boris reread more slowly. He stopped often to resettle his glasses on his broad Slavic features.

"Actually he writes obscenities about their last time together, and his plans for the next . . . he hopes the drugs he sent have arrived safely, and that she gets a good price on the black market. As I said, Major, it is all idle chatter, gossip . . ."

"Just fucking tell the Major what it says." Hyde shone the torch in the translator's face.

Boris did as he was told, hurriedly.

"He goes on to say that he will send her photographs they took in a refugee camp . . . they had used flame-throwers . . . he thinks she will find some of them funny. Here he says that he has not written for a while, as he was in detention for being drunk. He has been transferred

68

from the naval brigade to an independent company . . . that is all there is, it ends there."

"So now we know what we're up against." Revell accepted the return of the scraps and crushed them into his pocket. "Only Spetsnaz forces in the Warsaw Pact have naval brigades as well as independent companies."

"We had to come up against them sometime. The wonder is it hasn't occurred before this." Hyde could see that the information had upset Boris, but then any prospect of his falling back into the hands of the army he had deserted had that effect. For himself, he was well aware of the Russian elite forces reputation, but you could be just as dead from a bullet fired by a shit-scared dolt of an infantryman, as by a highly trained commando.

Unclipping his radio from his belt, Revell broadcast his call sign. As he waited for an acknowledgement, he looked again at the corpse on the tiled floor.

An outstretched hand seemed to reach towards the bundle of torn panels and rigging in a corner. It appeared almost a gesture of accusation, aimed at the chute that had failed him.

Briefly, Revell passed to control the information they had obtained. He signed off without waiting to hear their reaction. Not that there could be any doubt as to what it would be. At that very moment, the communication room in the bunker would have gone very quiet, as the news sank in.

Spetsnaz troops had an appalling record of atrocity, even gauged against the horrors that were everyday events in the Zone. This time though it was not helpless prisoners or even wretched refugees, this time they held a whole city in their bloodstained hands.

The police HQ had to be retaken quickly. Every weapon and every round the Special Combat Company could lay hands on was going to be needed in this fight.

CHAPTER TWELVE

The sniper fire from the area of the Karlstor Gate forced on Revell the decision to detour through the Stachus underground shopping mall. They lost two men in the dash from cover to the nearest of the pedestrian ramps.

It sloped gently. The textured nonslip surface rasped beneath their shuffling feet as they edged down towards the entrance.

Revell kept a grip on the handrail, straining his eyes to make sense of the shapes that loomed ahead. He could hear a growing noise, like a magnified restless murmur.

"What's the holdup?"

At the bottom of the ramp, the major caught up with Carrington and the scout section. The corporal was in a heated argument — conducted in hushed undertones — with an armed civilian wearing an auxiliary-police armband.

By the faint illumination of a well-shielded flashlight, Revell saw the German energetically shaking his head. While he did so, he managed to keep a rifle levelled at them, blocking the way through the heavy blackout curtain.

"This old fool says we can't go in. He says the place isn't an authorized shelter, and it's his job to keep everybody out. Shall I knock him down?" Carrington edged closer to the man as he asked.

Sensing rather than seeing her beside him, Revell told Andrea to speak to the sentry. "Tell him we know it's not a shelter. We don't want to stay in there, we simply want to cut through to reach the gunmen."

Though she spoke too fast for Revell to catch all that she said, he knew she was putting the point across more brutally than he had dictated.

The German took a nervous step back, but still kept the weapon aimed. He was opening his mouth to speak, when a fist caught him on the side of the face. His head cracked hard against the tiled wall, and he went down without uttering a sound.

Carrington caught the rifle as it fell. He rubbed his knuckles. "Boney little runt. I could have hurt my hand."

"Keep the rifle. Search him for ammunition." Revell took hold of the corner of the screening material. "Pass the word for every one to keep their wits about them. This place may be deserted, but it's like a rabbit warren. I've gotten lost when the lights were on."

Pushing through, Revell led the way into the complex of stores, and into a scene that could have come straight from a horror movie.

By the faintly glowing emergency lighting, he could see that every inch of floor space was occupied. Families and individuals sat or lay or slumped, as space about them dictated.

The air was hot, and stale with cigarette smoke and the reek of lager, vomit, and urine. Close inside the entrance, the floor was slippery with blood, and several imperfectly shrouded bodies lay there.

In a nearby corner two men were propped against a poster-decorated wall. Improvised bandages swathed their bare chests and supported their smashed jaws. Both were moaning and whimpering in pain.

The strangely sibilant sound that Revell had been only partially aware of, now grew in volume as the huddled masses of civilians recognized the newcomers.

From one woman came shrieks of fear as she mistook

71

the NATO battle dress and weapons for Russian. Others hissed her to a sobbing silence.

"What the bloody hell was that old fool on about, not letting anyone in." Sergeant Hyde surveyed the crowd. "There must be thousands here."

"But they didn't get in through *his* entrance." It was a peculiar mentality that Revell had encountered before in West Germany. It seemed to be compounded of devotion to the rule book and pigheaded stubbornness.

As they moved forward, they were bombarded with questions and pleas from all sides. Further in, the press about them became worse, and Revell had to call Dooley up to the point, to force a way through.

In the confined space the hubbub grew to a head-aching din that nothing could quiet. The plate glass storefronts and their bright goods reflected such slight illumination as there was, mostly from ornate candles looted from a gift counter. Their flicker gave faces a spectral appearance that deepened the lines of worry and fear they displayed.

From a distant recess came singing and shouting, discordant and guttural. The blare of a portable cassette player carried clearly, but failed to drown the calls and pleas of the mob.

A beer can rolled away from Hyde's boots, to be instantly trampled flat by the crush. "It'll only take a fight among a handful of drunks to start a rush for the exits. Where the hell are the police?"

They passed an entrance to a subway. Surrounding it was a scrum of struggling people packed so tightly most could hardly move. Everyone who had seen what a death trap the shallow glass-filled mall would be in an air raid was trying to reach the greater safety of the rapid transit system.

Several caught among the throng looked terrified. Their eyes bulged, all color had drained from their faces. Hyde was reminded of the appearance of the bodies he'd seen hauled from the tangle of dead at the other subway entrance.

Even as he noted the similarity, he saw a tall blonde woman in the middle of the crowd close her eyes and loll against those about her. As the mass shuffled and surged back and forth, she sank gradually lower until she was lost from sight.

There was nothing he could do. It would have taken the united efforts of the whole company to bring some degree of order to the mad scramble. The odd one or two at the back who did give up were instantly replaced by others prepared to try.

He didn't like to think what it would be like lower down, in the passageways and on the stalled escalators. On the platforms, furious fights would be taking place as those already safe resisted the efforts of others to replace them.

The flashlight beam moved on to fresh scenes as they skirted the heaving jam of people. With every step they took, hands reached out of the crowd to try to detain them. It was as though their owners hoped to pluck answers to a hundred different questions from their sleeves.

Many of the accompanying voices conveyed anger, others terror. The majority had a sharp hysterical edge. None were satisfied, and they tried the same interrogation of one soldier after another as they filed past.

Twice Revell located exits, to find below them dead and dying who had already tried—and failed—to leave by those routes. Everywhere the Russian snipers appeared to be waiting.

It was Garrett who discovered a service stairway, when he stepped aside to search the scattered cartons of a kiosk in the hope of finding a candy bar.

A padlocked steel grill barred their path. It did not resist their combined efforts for long. A hinge twisted and tore from the frame with a gunshotlike crack. Quelling the local panic it created took several anxious moments.

The staircase spiralled as it climbed steeply. Revell could hear the quiet cursing of the men behind him, as he followed the silently moving scout section.

"So where the hell are we?" First to reach the head of the stairs, Ripper looked out into the narrow service road it connected with. He crouched low, using the cover of a stack of empty crates.

Carrington joined him. The rear of a building further along looked vaguely familiar.

"If that's the rear of the multistorey car park that I think it is, then we're in the same block as the puppet theatre. That's a bit north of Karlstor Gate. Looks like we've had a slice of luck, and come out in the right place."

"And since when have you been into marionettes, Corporal?" Garrett pushed the machine gun out through the door and sighted it in the direction of the Stachus. "Thought you liked more grownup entertainments than that."

Ripper dived across the alleyway and into the concealment of wheeled garbage bins on the far side.

"Spent the week with a girl who's got a couple of kids." Carrington waited to see if there was any reaction, before waving Ripper to move on cautiously. "So most of the days we spent as a foursome, didn't we."

"Sounds fun." Garrett thought of his own seven days. It had been a week of restless drifting from one tatty hotel to another, hoping to pick up a girl, anybody. He'd wandered the streets in the evenings until he'd got fed up. To dull the boredom he'd look for oblivion in the nearest cheap bar, and usually find it. Shit, any week had to be more fun than that. Even having a couple of brats in tow had to be more fun.

74

"Have you orientated yourself, Corporal?"

"I know the area, Major. Been dragged this way on a couple of shopping expeditions recently."

"Right, then get us to St. Michael's Church. We'll want to get in the back way, not off the pedestrian precinct. You know it?"

"Opposite the police station? Big fat block of a building. Loads of statues all over the front."

"That's it."

"What if the Reds are inside?"

"I don't think they will be. They're spread thin on the ground. If they are holding the police HQ, then I can't see them also holding the place virtually next to it. They might be in the twin towers of the cathedral on the far side though, so keep us out of the line of sight of those."

Revell watched the scouts move out. He allowed an interval, and then fed the rest of the company through the doorway after them.

When Sgt. Hyde came up with the rearguard, some civilians were already close behind them and had to be held back.

For a brief moment the major tried to remonstrate with their leaders, but it was no use. About twenty dashed off in either direction as soon as their exit was no longer obstructed.

"Poor bloody fools." Hyde shouldered his machine pistol. "It wasn't nice down there, but it's got to be safer than running about up here."

As he spoke, the first of the civilians who had gone that way reached the junction of the alleyway and the broad open space before the Karlstor Gate. Shots and screams blended as they were mowed down.

CHAPTER THIRTEEN

Swirling clouds of white tear gas issued from the broken windows of the police headquarters. From the upper floors and rooftops of surrounding buildings came shotgun blasts that shattered more panes. After each would come another shower of the canisters. They would burst and fill yet another room or staircase with their choking fumes.

Dislodged and torn blackout curtains let light escape, forming a series of pearly halos. A few rounds missed their goals. Those grenades rolled in the gutter, wreathing the ground floor and roadway in the chemical fog, adding to the ghostly effect.

There had been a smattering of returned fire to the initial assault. It had petered out in the absence of identifiable targets, fallen to no more than an occasional random shot.

Leading the first attack group, Hyde rushed his men from the church, through the thickest of the smoke screen and into a small courtyard. Several police vehicles were parked there. They took cover among them.

Above the archway by which they had entered, and on the other three sides of the enclosure, the building rose to three or four floors. All windows at ground level were barred. Many had frosted glass.

Several doors led off the courtyard. Tentatively tried, all were found to be locked or barricaded.

Looking back, Hyde saw Revell's assault group racing through the open gates. There wasn't going to be sufficient concealment for all of them in the confined space. If they were spotted, it would be instantly turned into a killing ground.

Straight ahead was the heavy double door the major had briefed him about. He waved Ripper and Ackerman forward.

Standing braced to either side of the large cast-brass handles, both men fired together. Smoke and splinters flew thickly about them as they fired twice more.

A combined shoulder charge by Dooley and Burke caved in the shattered timber. They threw themselves flat as blasts of automatic fire were sent up the corridor running away to left and right.

The respirator keeping out the effects of the gas didn't mask the smell of the gunsmoke as Revell moved quickly inside. Not much of the irritant had yet found its way to this quarter of the building.

He knew the armory was on the top floor. The cloud of gas would grow thicker as they moved upwards and towards the front of the building. That was where the brunt of the barrage was taking place.

After the hours of darkness, it seemed strangely unreal to be in a well-lit building. Holding up his hand for silence, Revell listened for any clue to the whereabouts or the approach of the Russians. There was only the sound of his own breathing, muted by the filtering mask over his face.

Pausing only to let those men who would accompany him reload, the major moved onward. The building was an enormous maze. If he posted men to guard every intersecting corridor, then before he was on the third floor, he'd be on his own. The alternative was to search every room as they went. There was not the time nor the manpower to do that.

Finding the short flight of stairs that he'd been looking for, Revell started up. At its top, glass double doors opened into a broad passageway that ran the length of the building. He knew it would be covered.

Try as he could, he couldn't remember which way the doors opened — inwards towards the stairs or out into the corridor. He was scrutinizing them, endeavoring to judge by the way the hinges were mounted, when he noticed the gap between them.

Visible for only a tiny fraction of its length, a filament of fire wire bridged the gap on the side away from him. Signalling the others back, Revell edged down the stairs until the barrel of his pump gun rested on the top tread. He lined it up, ducked low, and squeezed the trigger.

The report of the firing was drowned by the roar of the detonating boobytrap grenade as the doors burst open. A mad hail of glass, wood, and plaster smothered them. Before it had begun to settle, Revell was leading his men through the wreckage.

No shots came, and they crouched low, hugging the walls as they waited for the smoke to clear. It did so to reveal two bodies. Both — a man and a woman — were in police uniforms.

The woman's was close enough for Ripper to reach out and touch. Cautiously he rolled the body over. Dust from the explosion failed to hide the closely spaced holes across face and neck.

"Not our doing."

"Never mind them. We keep moving."

Dashing to the next staircase, Revell sent a blast from his shotgun straight up it, then stepped aside. Other members of the team fired baton rounds against the wall at its top.

The cylinders of plastic deformed on impact and whirled away to right and left. For a few precious seconds, anyone who waited up there in ambush for them would be either flat on the floor taking cover, or knocked down

78

and in no state to fight.

Flanked by submachine gunners, Revell went up two steps at a time. As he reached the top, a bullet smacked plaster from the wall beside him. He turned to see a Russian paratrooper being hurled backwards by the impact of the contents of a magazine.

Revell stripped the body of three fragmentation and one stun grenade, even as it made its last twitching movements.

Through fire doors at the far end of a corridor another figure appeared. A Kalashnikov was levelled and already spitting bullets.

Shotguns and automatics blazed a return fire, and the Russian was almost torn apart by the multiple impacts. He crashed to the floor, flailing in his death throes.

Darting in to retrieve another stunbomb clipped to the dying man's webbing, Revell found himself at the foot of yet another set of stairs. He noticed them at the same instant he saw a grenade tumbling down towards him.

Lunging forward, he caught it before its final impact, and thrust it under the partially dismembered body beside him. Throwing himself aside, he was only a couple of meters away when it detonated.

The corpse was lifted by the blast. Blood and intestines spattered the walls and ceiling. Revell felt himself being shoved sideways by the shock wave. His respirator was torn from his face. He wasn't aware of any noise, and thought for an instant his eardrums had been burst. Then he was helped to his feet, and knew that wasn't the case when their machine roared into action beside him.

Firing a fifty-round belt from the hip, in precise ten-round bursts, Dooley sent ball- and armor-piercing rounds through the walls flanking the head of the stairs.

A paratrooper clutching an AK47 staggered into view. Blood streamed from his face. Taking a grenade from his still-dazed officer, Hyde lobbed it to land beside the man.

Pulling his mask back on, Revell felt the wall against which he leant jolt hard against him. He was aware of men rushing past, of the sound of intensive exchanges of fire. Then there came the concussion of two more grenade explosions.

Retrieving his shotgun from the floor, Revell found he still had the use of all his limbs, though his wrist was numb where he'd jarred it on his heavy landing. Apart from general bruising and a ringing in his ears, he appeared to have suffered no injury.

The pieces of flesh littering the corridor told him how very different it could have been.

On the floor above, the firing had ceased. He made his way to that level. It was to find a scene of far worse carnage than that he'd left.

Component parts of several bodies were scattered about. Blood drenched every surface and ran in sluggish rivulets across the polished tile floor. Lumps of tissue slid slowly down every wall and adhered to the cracked plaster overhead. There was an appalling stench from the spilled contents of several stomachs and bowels.

One of his own men lay dead, shot through the chest. A high velocity bullet had penetrated his flak vest, passed clean through, and exited below his neck. The collar of his body armor had been ripped off. Another man was having a rough splint bound about a shattered arm. He smiled vaguely through a morphia-induced haze.

"That seems to have accounted for them all, Major." Hyde indicated a makeshift barricade.

A severed arm lay across the top of a shrapnel-holed filing cabinet. From beneath a collapsed pile of word processors, projected a pair of legs, incongruously naked except for their paratrooper boots. It would have taken more than that to add humor to the scene.

"Just the two casualties?"

"If you're okay, yes, Major." Hyde had been taking in the officer's torn and blood-soaked battle dress.

"This isn't mine, I'm happy to say. Have the building searched from top to bottom, every room. I don't think it's likely, but one of them might just be holed up, waiting for us to drop our guard."

"Something you should see in here, Major."

Ripper came out of a side room. Revell noticed the look on his face and asked no questions, going to see for himself.

There were about thirty bodies in the little office. Most were in police uniform, several women among them. They showed clear evidence of having been mown down by automatic fire from the doorway.

Burke trudged up the stairs as they came out of the room. "Just checked the cell block, Major. Five dead police down there. The prisoners are all okay. Still locked up tight."

"Find the keys. Get them up here." Revell looked about at the mess. "They can clear the place up. We'll have to leave a defending force here. No reason why they should have to walk back and forth through this. Now let's find that armory."

Hyde followed. "I hope it's well stocked. This was only the start."

CHAPTER FOURTEEN

The first light of dawn was in the sky as the hunting team left police headquarters. There was no shortage of weapons now, nor of ammunition.

In the armory they had discovered an Aladdin's cave, containing every infantry weapon that had for so long been in short supply in the Zone itself. Rack after rack had been filled with small arms. Also there had been several cases of assorted grenades and a batch of anti-tank rockets.

Revell had spent some minutes musing over what Those last items had been doing there. They were hardly standard issue to any police force, not even SWAT teams. He could only think they were there in case the police found themselves having to put down a revolt by army units. It was not a nice thought, that such things had to be planned for, but he knew it to be necessary. It had happened in Hanover once. Only quick action by the police had stopped a rebellion by a French infantry unit.

He'd insisted that all the men rearm with Heckler and Koch MP5 submachine guns, to replace the assorted ar-morment they had obtained from the transport police. Their greater accuracy at their maximum effective range would be a useful asset in the wide streets and broad plazas of the city.

So too would its thirty-percent faster rate of fire, when it came to close quarters engagements. And the high capacity magazine was another point in the weapon's favor.

Intending to leave only a couple of sections to hold the police HQ, Revell had been less than happy to be ordered to leave most of his force there. He wasn't told as much, but it appeared likely that everyone would be transferring from the bunker as soon as conditions permitted. They wanted to be quite certain it would stay in their hands until the switch was made.

There was no way Revell was about to accept a garrison roll for himself. He intended to lead the two sections he'd been able to detach to assist in the clearing-up operation. That was how he found himself with them as they made for their first objective.

The target was a building close by the Theatiner Church near Odeons Platz. From it snipers were dominating the road junction and the entrances to a dozen large shelters.

"You think they know what they're doing?" Hyde maintained his position a few paces behind the officer as they hugged the storefronts.

"What I think is that the generals are interfering, trying to run the operation by committee." Moving quickly from cover to cover, Revell had no intention of giving any sniper a clear shot or the time to take it.

"Should be exciting then, when those special forces units arrive." Hyde shrank back into a doorway as the scouts signalled a warning. "At the moment when quick thinking will be called for, they'll be going into a huddle and voting on motions and amendments."

There was the sound of breaking glass further along the road. Then there came an indistinct crunching noise, like someone was walking on broken glass. For a brief while there came a scuffling, rummaging sound, and then the rapid patter of running feet.

"Looters. Let them go. The police can have them, we're not here for that."

Two young men in trainers and tracksuits came

sprinting down the sidewalk. Trying to keep up with them was a girl. All of them had their arms full of small electrical goods.

Seeing the patrol ahead of them, the men hesitated, turned, and went to cut across the road. The girl followed, losing more ground as she was slowed by having to zigzag between parked cars.

Both men were hit by a burst of fire. They threw their arms in the air, scattering their goods, and were spun around by the impacts of the soft-nosed Soviet bullets. Expanding, dumdum fashion, they had an explosive effect, tearing flesh open and destroying the tissue beneath.

Neither was killed outright. While one of them kicked wildly, threshing about in his extreme agony, the other lay paralyzed. A fountain of blood spouted from his mouth, to splash audibly on the wheel of a Volkswagen.

"Keep down." Revell shouted to the girl.

In her unreasoning fear at the shock of what she was witnessing, she had stopped. Unable to take her eyes off the horrific sights in the road, she froze.

She was too far away. Revell knew he could never reach her in time.

The reality of the situation appeared to strike her, and she threw down the loot. Revell was sure she was going to turn and run, but she didn't. In a trancelike state, visibly shaking, she started towards the sniper's victims.

Scanning the buildings opposite, Revell calculated that the origin of the fire had to be one of the second-floor windows of a small hotel. To an inch he could estimate when she would be within the sniper's field of fire.

"All weapons. The hotel, second floor. Fire." As an example, Revell blasted off a whole magazine. He had to fight to keep the tip of the muzzle down, as the escaping gasses forced it to climb away from the aiming point.

84

Twenty other submachine guns and two rocket launchers unleashed a storm of steel and high explosive. Two hundred meters off, the facade of the hotel seemed to dissolve in a cloud of dust and fragments of brickwork.

The first of the larger projectiles struck immediately below a window. Vivid red and yellow flame climbed in a bubble up the front of the structure.

Soaring in through the smoke created by the first, the second rocket detonated in the heart of the building. A blow torch of flame jetted across the street.

Heedless of what was happening about her, the girl reached the men. One of them had died, but the other still moved convulsively. She bent towards him, her hand reaching out hesitantly.

A single shot punched into her hip, and she collapsed with a cry of pain and distress. Her fingers ran down her side until they encountered the deep hole created, and the pulped flesh within it. Her screams went so high as to almost go off the audible scale.

Under covering fire, Sampson scrambled low behind the parked vehicles, until he could reach the closest gap and dash out through it to reach her.

As he grabbed her by the collar of her jacket, another shot was aimed at them. It struck the road a little short and ricochetted up underneath the girl. She bucked at the impact and then writhed, making it hard for him to keep his grip.

Another single round drilled through the skull of the wounded man, and he was suddenly still.

Fire from the MP5s continued to drench the suspected building in a hail of lead. By sheer volume alone it was successful in suppressing the enemy attention.

No more bullets came their way, as Sampson dragged the girl to cover.

"Shit. How am I supposed to put a dressing down

there?" Cutting away the girl's jeans, Sampson examined the damage created by the second shot.

"You better do something. She's bleeding real bad." Ripper looked at the nearest of the stores. "I've got an idea."

He tackled the plate glass of a drapers with the butt of his submachine gun. It finally shattered, and he was able to reach into the display. Selecting a pack of bed sheets, he tossed them to the medic.

"Here, try these."

"Too late to be any help. We lost her. Don't think there was anything we could have done." Sampson sat back on his heels beside the body.

"I hope the police roadblocks keep the tourists and opportunists out of the city." Hyde covered the staring face. "If they don't, there are going to be a lot more like her."

"There's still an air raid warning in force." Garrett avoided looking at the girl's torn and mangled lower torso. "No one is going to be so stupid as to try and come in before the all-clear, are they?"

"A lot will have been on their way here overnight by road." That was a point worrying Revell no less than Stadler. "They'll be coming in by all the back routes to avoid the expected traffic. There's no obvious signs of damage to warn them off."

Hyde watched Sampson draw a sheet over the body. It was instantly drenched in blood. "If they haven't heard anything on the radio, and manage to avoid all the checkpoints, there'll be nothing to stop them."

"Maybe this is the first." Dooley pointed to the far end of the street.

A BMW coupe, headlamps blazing, was accelerating fast towards them. Straight into the sniper's killing ground.

CHAPTER FIFTEEN

A glance at the hotel from which the fire had come re-assured Revell. It was well alight. Flames sprouted from several windows, and the canopies above were flaring brightly in the early morning light. The sniper must have been driven out.

The BMW did not check its speed as it closed on the rolling bank of smoke coming from the side street. Revell sent Dooley forward to flag it down, but even as he stepped off the curb, a weapon was aimed from a rear window and a wild burst was sprayed in his direction.

Dooley threw himself behind the parked cars, looking back to the major to see if he should return the fire. Before Revell could make that decision, the BMW was almost level with them.

Hyde had noted the inexperienced way in which the coupe was handled, was ready to fire, anticipating the command, but it didn't come. It wasn't needed.

Doing close to a hundred, the driver noticed the bodies in the roadway just too late. Throwing the wheel over, he tried to slalom around the prone forms. Broad tires being stripped of tread and squealing under the forces imposed on them, the BMW clipped the tailboard of a truck parked at an angle to the curb.

A fender was crushed into a wheel, and with its windshield shattered by the collision, the car went out of control. There was a succession of further impacts as the BMW wrecked a line of vehicles by concertinaing them. Then came a last torrent of noise as it pounded into, and partly demolished, the porch of a bank.

Steam gushed from the battered car as Hyde and Dooley tugged at its jammed doors. The driver's side came open and an AK47 clattered out on to the road.

"Spetsnaz." Reaching in through a glassless back window, Hyde retrieved a holdall from the crushed back seat. Delving into it, he pulled out a handful of assorted gold jewelry, then a second, then a third. "These boys were going freelance."

As the steam and dust of the impact drifted clear, Revell could see that the three men in the coupe all wore Soviet paratroop coveralls and helmets. The crumpled floor was littered deeply with more jewelry and loose ammunition.

One of the three Russians was still alive. He was dragged out, semiconscious. Both his arms were obviously broken at wrist and elbow, where he had tried to brace himself by holding onto the back of the front seats. His face was covered in blood from a broken nose and more dripped down his front from his mouth.

Sampson pulled the man's bottom jaw down, and more blood poured out. "Don't hold out and hopes of interrogating this guy, Major." Sampson bent down for a closer look. "He's gone and bitten his tongue clean through. Must have some internal injuries as well, judging by the difficulty he's having breathing."

Propped against the side of the wreck, the Russian groaned as he tried to move his arms. His eyes were open startlingly wide, but he appeared to be looking through the men, unseeing. His mouth hung slack, blood pulsing from the back of his throat. Again in his pain he made a slight movement.

His left eye splattered apart as a shot rang out. The other closed abruptly, and a strong pulse of blood became instantly a trickle that soon stopped.

"He was going for a weapon." Andrea saw the looks directed her as she holstered her pistol.

"Like hell he was." Revell had been all but deafened by the report almost in his ear. "With two broken wrists?"

Andrea shrugged. "What would you have done? Bound his injuries and sent him for treatment? This way we waste no time on him."

There was nothing, Revell knew, that he could say that would get through to her. The fact that the Russian was probably dying made no difference. If she could have cut short his life by half a second, then Andrea would have done it. The only time he had ever seen her spare a Russian who she could have finished, was when they were trapped in burning vehicles.

Dooley was looking longingly at the gold bracelets and rings brightening the gory interior of the BMW "Nice stuff, but it wouldn't have gone far between three of them. Suppose they couldn't resist it, never having seen anything like it back home."

"You are very wrong about their not having seen such goods before." Boris had been looking for ways to fill his own pockets, but was aware that Sgt. Hyde was watching him. He was also very aware of Andrea being close by. He knew that only the major's presence prevented her from summarily executing him. "But correct about them not seeing such things in the USSR. Many Spetsnaz, like KGB men, travelled widely in the West before the war. Usually as members of sports teams. It helped them get to know their future targets."

"So this lot will have already done a reconnaissance of Munich, got to know the ground." Dooley reluctantly tossed a heavy gate-bracelet back into the wreck. "Pity they didn't teach them to drive decently at the same time."

As usual, Boris took the remark quite seriously at face value. "I do not think that instruction on a Moskvitch or

Lada is good training for handling a BMW, but that and army vehicles is all they would have had."

It was quite light now, and with the day was coming more evidence of attempts to tackle the Russian incursion. Small-arms fire could be heard coming from several directions. Some was clearly sniper fire, single shots at widely spaced intervals. That would mark enemy attempts to keep the civilians below ground. But there were also outbreaks of heavier exchanges, proof that police units were also getting involved on an organized scale.

As yet, there was nothing to indicate that the columns supposed to be working their way inwards, were as yet anywhere nearby. Revell hadn't expected that there would be by this time, if there was to be any at all.

If Col. Klee's men had his enthusiasm for their task, they might not even have left their barracks yet. As for the force coming in from the airport, their antiterrorist training hardly fitted them for the role of streetfighting infantry. It was likely their progress would be very slow.

Re-forming the patrol, Revell had a brief word with control — to advise them of the burning hotel and the casualties — and then resumed their interrupted progress.

Every intersection, every open space, and every wide avenue was a potential death trap, but taking to side roads wherever they could, they encountered no more snipers.

There were more bodies to be seen. Individual police officers, emergency service vehicles with their crews dead in and around them, and a surprising number of civilians.

Most were near the entrances to air raid shelters. A few were scattered more widely. Some could be identified as looters by the goods they still clutched in a last greedy embrace. Others were there for less definable reasons. Perhaps they were drunks who had not heeded the sirens,

90

or possibly the more desperate of the many who found the shelters hard to endure.

Revell didn't know how many shelters there were, but there had to be quite a number the enemy gunmen did not cover. From them would come a steady trickle of the more foolish or foolhardy. Perhaps the obvious sounds of conflict would convince the majority to stay under cover, even though no bombing had materialized.

Ahead of them there appeared to be a fierce firefight in progress. Halting, Revell tried by radio to determine if any SWAT team was already engaging their objective. He didn't believe, until they had checked twice, that none of the units under the city's control were fighting in the area.

"Maybe it's two Spetsnaz mobs slugging it out with each other?" Hyde tried to identify the weapons in use by their rates of fire, but so many were being employed it was impossible to single out any individual.

Carrington came loping back from the point. "This is about as close as we're going to get, Major. You could walk on the lead that's flying about down there."

"Okay, so find me a vantage point. I want to have a look for myself. We're not going to stroll into any cross-fire."

"There's the church tower."

A spent round zipped past. Two more followed, bursting scabs of soft stone from a door post.

"I hope that tower is well made." Revell felt to check that his flak vest was fastened.

As they started forward, the gunfire ahead seemed to increase in volume and ferocity.

CHAPTER SIXTEEN

They had no trouble entering the church, a side door was open. But officer and NCO were not prepared for what they found there.

It was full. Every seat, every bit of space in the aisles, even right up to the alter rail the church was crammed with people. A thousand pairs of eyes looked at them as they entered, and followed them as they made their way, with difficulty, towards the tower staircase.

"No, you must leave."

A priest ran towards them, tripping frequently on the outstretched legs of his overspilling congregation.

"Please, do not bring the fighting in here, not in God's own house, I beg you."

He grabbed both men by their arms and tried to turn them. Men among the crowd got to their feet and looked likely to add their efforts.

Revell shook himself free and unslung his submachine gun. "Why aren't these people in the shelters, or at least down in the crypt?"

With the gun being cradled, the cleric and his would-be helpers fell back. They watched the weapon as much as the major.

"The crypt is full, but these people came here for more than mere shelter. Please, do not bring the fighting in here."

The gunfight outside had not diminished in intensity, but its crash and clatter was muted by the thick walls. There was multicolored glass on the floor, where stray bullets had punched through the high-set stained glass windows.

"We're not here to set up a fire base. All we want is to use the tower as an observation post, for a very short while."

Partly reassured, the priest still looked uncertain.

"I doubt we'll be in here more than a couple of minutes."

"But you may be seen, and then the guns will be turned on these people. Look at them, they have been through so much already."

Revell *had* been looking at them. Going by their faces, he could see little proof that any of them had found the comfort they had come here for. On every side, tired faces watched him intently, showing their concentration as they strained to catch what was being said. Some were already gathering their belongings together.

The priest saw those actions and turned aside to urge the crowd to stay. The packing was halted, but not undone.

"If you show us the best spot, there will be less chance of our being seen, and we'll be on our way all the sooner. We're trying to stop what's going on out there."

"Very well, I will. But please, will you leave your weapons by the door?"

There was no way Revell could or would comply with the request. Among the faces of the frightened faithful — and those who had suddenly, if perhaps temporarily, found their faith again — he had noticed several distinctly un-Christian faces. Bulky packs and parcels, carefully guarded by the rough individuals, strongly suggested to Revell that some looters had found the church a convenient bolt hole when the fighting had swept to this quarter.

"I'll give mine to my corporal. He'll wait down here."

Seeing that was the best arrangement he could make, the priest led the way to a low doorway and up a steep and winding set of stone steps.

As they climbed, the sounds of battle grew louder, when on a landing where a shutter was pulled fractionally open, it burst upon them at full volume.

The intersection, with its wide expanse of pedestrian pavement, was spread out below him. Masses of tracer were converging on a corner property off to Revell's right. It came mostly from a long building across the way. There was hardly a window in it that was not the source of a near-continuous stream of light-automatic fire.

Moving to another side of the tower, Revell looked in vain for any sign of answering fire from the structure being gradually chipped and flaked to a ruin by the hail of bullets.

"Okay, I've seen enough. I know what we're up against."

"Thank God." Securing the shutters, the priest hurried after Revell.

Retrieving his weapon, Revell was about to leave when the priest restrained him.

"I know that if I ask you to put down your guns and implore you to stay, you would not. So I can only hope it is your sense of duty and not a lust for killing that sends you back to that terrible fighting. Before that, join me in prayer."

"I'm sorry." Strangely, for an instant, Revell almost felt inclined to do just that.

"So am I, for your sake. At least, think of some words of the Lord as you go."

From deep inside his memory came words that Revell had not heard for a long time, to which he'd never given thought. *Thou shalt not kill* . . . He said them quietly, almost to himself.

"Yes, *man soll nicht toten*. It is not too late to stop killing. It is never too late."

"It's been too late for me for a long time, Father."

The priest watched them go. Overhead another fragment of colored glass, in an already damaged window, was splintered to a thousand pieces that rained into his vestments. He turned to the alter. "Then I shall say it for you."

The interior of the Residence was magnificent, but Revell had no time for its rich decorations and furnishings as he led a squad through its long halls and high-ceilinged apartments.

"Fucking hell, look at this lot." Dooley paused beside a long glass-topped showcase. It held row after row of neatly labelled silver coins.

Reluctantly he kept up with the others, as they passed many more cases containing the city's famous coin collection.

"This stuff must be worth a fortune." He kept attempting to snatch glances at the displays. "You think they'd have shifted it out of the city, what with the Zone being right on their doorstep."

"A lot *has* been moved; they've had copies made." Burke checked that he had a round chambered. They were right underneath the floor from which the massed firing was emanating. He could hear empty cartridge cases raining down on a tiled floor. "I suppose they've been trying to keep the city as normal as possible for as long as possible. This little lot should blow the lid off that, I imagine."

"Where are you going? You can't come through here, get out, get out."

"Not again." Revell wasn't prepared to go through another sermon.

A fussily officious little man in an attendant's uniform had bounced out of a side room, almost getting himself shot by Ripper.

"Shit, you got a death wish?"

Wagging his finger at them, the security man kept up with their rapid pace through the building. "You cannot come in here, the Residence is closed."

An old steel helmet—too small even over his thin face—perched on his head, giving him the appearance of an image stretched in a distorting mirror.

"Fuck off, grandad, there's a war on." Dooley brushed an attempt at obstruction aside.

Still the German skittered along with them, using a peculiar, hopping crablike motion as he persisted in his efforts to halt their progress.

"The Residence is closed." His voice hit a high falsetto, and he flew in to a passionate rage at being ignored. "Closed, closed, *closed.*"

"Right, it's closed. Pretend we're not here." Burke gave the old man a gentle push.

The move caught him off balance, and he fell back, to land hard on his bottom. Lost for words, he went bright red and beat his fists on the floor.

At the end of the gallery, high folding doors opened out onto a movie-style marble staircase with glittering gilded handrails. There was no need for them to exercise caution as they started up. The noise of the gunfire coming from the top floor was deafening and nonstop.

Reaching the top, Revell indicated a doorway to Sgt. Hyde. "All yours."

Slinging his submachine gun, Hyde stepped into the opening and drew a deep breath.

"Cease fire. Fucking cease fire."

CHAPTER SEVENTEEN

In a reflex response to the bellowed command, twenty uniformed figures leapt back from the windows.

Not giving the surprised machine-gunners time to recover, Hyde employed his drill-sergeant bellow once more. "Make your weapons safe."

"Thank you, Sergeant." Revell entered the long room. At his every step, cartridge cases rolled under his feet.

"Jesus, it's bloody women."

Dooley and the rest of the squad paused in the doorway, and gawped as they took in the scene.

Revell walked to the nearest window and looked out at the building across the way. Its stonework had a kind of stippled finish from the number of rounds that had sprayed it. Every window and frame was shattered, and every piece of external ornamentation had been shot away, as had the downspouts.

"Who's in charge?" He hadn't been expecting any, but Revell was relieved all the same when he withdrew his head without it attracting any fire.

"Actually we all are, sort of, sir. Only I'm the most senior, by six days, so really I suppose I am. Private Sharon Henson reporting, sir."

"At ease. Do you mind telling me what you were shooting at, and where you got all this ammunition?"

"There are, there *were* Russian paratroops in the offices overlooking the intersection. The guns and ammunition we had in the armory at our headquarters. It's just down the road a little way."

"So, who gave you your orders?" Revell looked over the women. They were of all ages, all builds, and all were

97

nervous, now that the adrenalin of action was draining away.

"We're here on our own initiative, sir, Major."

"Any casualties?"

Private Henson looked down. "Just one, she's over at the back."

Sending Sampson to investigate, Revell swept a mass of cartridges aside with his boot. "No men in your HQ, no officers?"

"Only the guard detail, Major. They wanted to come along, but we thought it best they stay there. They'd have been deserting their post. We happened to be working a late shift. The officer had gone back to quarters."

"The lady bought it, Major." Sampson handed dog tags to Henson. "You better have these. Must have been real fast."

"She was leaning out to get a better shot. We got excited and forgot what we'd been taught."

"It was the fact that I could see the tips of the barrels resting on the sills that told me you weren't Spetsnaz. You should have been firing from further back inside the room. We'd best have a look at what sort of a job you've done."

The women all crowded forward to go with him.

"No, not all of you, just a couple. The rest of you, get some showcases and set them up just in from the windows. Rest the weapons on those. And find a few chairs or benches, something strong to stand on, so you can fire down into the street without showing yourselves."

"Wonder how long they'd have gone on firing if we hadn't turned up?" Ackerman had been leering at a plump girl who busied herself with gathering the submachine guns together and pointedly ignored him.

"They've still got a few more cases of ammo." Dooley watched with amusement as one of the women produced a broom from somewhere and began to sweep up the brass cases. "Until it was all gone, or that place fell down, I suppose."

A touch was all that was needed to push down the stout oak door at the entrance to the office block. The timber had been gouged from the hinges, leaving just the tips of the screws still holding it up, and the lock had been burst and battered.

The fall of the door brought down a set of stepladders just inside, and a large pot of paint was thrown down to splash its contents over the dust sheets partially covering the carpet.

"This will upset someone." Hyde skirted the sluggish puddle of eggshell blue. "Looks like they'd almost finished refurbishing the place."

Carrington and his team went ahead, while Revell looked cautiously into the ground-floor rooms. All the walls that faced the windows were liberally sprinkled with bullet holes. Once smart lined curtains were now slashed and bedraggled tatters. They smoldered gently where tiny pieces of phosphorus had lodged in them.

At a call from Carrington, Revell led the two women to the third floor. At the head of the stairs lay two bodies. Both were smothered in blood. Nearby was a broken Kalashnikov rifle.

Sampson knelt by the corpses. "Hey, those little girls are dead shots. Both through the head."

"Look again."

"I'm not mistaken, Major, but if you say so." Sampson turned and prodded the bodies. "Hot shit. Sorry ladies. Hell, will you look at that."

On the first Russian, Sampson pulled at his camouflage jacket and pointed to a neat puncture wound immediately below the rib cage on the right-hand side.

"No exit wound, but from the position, I'd say that

99

went clean through his liver. The man was dying." He turned to the second body.

This time he had had to look harder, but he found what he knew the major had expected him to look for. "Must have been a ricochet to get him through the leg. That would have been below the window level. It's broken alright. He wouldn't be going anywhere in a hurry."

"They're shooting their wounded, that's horrible!" Sharon put her hands to her face and stared at the remains. "How can they do that? They could have lived, with treatment. Certainly one of them would."

"They're indoctrinated to think of cruelty as a virtue. By those standards, this would have been almost maudlin." Revell walked through the rooms. In an alcove behind a big old-fashioned photocopier, he found what he was looking for.

A pile of brick and plaster debris, below a ragged man-sized hole in the wall, showed where the rest of the Russian squad had mouse-holed out of this building and into the next. He could be confident that if they investigated they would find a similar thing in there, and very likely in the building after that. By this time they would be far away. Pursuit would be pointless, and dangerous. There had to be a strong possibility that the escape route would be mined. That he would happily leave to the experts to deal with.

"Sgt. Hyde." Until he caught sight of an empty soup carton, Revell had not even thought of food. Now he realized he was hungry. "Do you know anywhere close by where we can help ourselves to a bite? Doesn't have to be anything fancy. So long as it's likely to have a well-stocked fridge."

The question showed how little the major knew about Hyde's life outside of the Zone. With his fire-ravaged facial disfigurement, he'd hardly been out at all during their week in the city. During the day he'd stayed in his room, watching television. If he did go out, it was at night, away from the well-frequented quarters. What sort of fancy restaurant would have even let him through the door, to frighten the clientele.

"I'll ask Carrington; he's been out and about."

"No need, Sarge." Ackerman had given up trying to get a quick grope with either of the women. "What sort of grub do you want? Chinese, Turkish, Indian—"

"We want the sort you don't have to cook." Revell cut short the recital. "In case you haven't noticed, everyone is down the shelters. There are no chefs waiting for us to march in and order."

"Got just the place, Major. Right around the corner, close by the Hof Garden."

"That'll do. Sergeant, tell Garrett to report in our new position. We'll see the women back safely on the way. The city seems fairly quiet at the moment."

"Lull before the storm perhaps." Hyde began to herd the men downstairs. "I think I prefer it when I can hear shooting coming from all over. At least then we know that not all the Reds are hanging about around here."

Ackerman pushed past others to get into the lead. He felt like rubbing his hands. He never imagined he'd have stood a chance to make money out of a day like this.

He'd managed to pocket a few trinkets from the haul the Russians had stashed in the getaway car. Now he was set to make a handful of cash. Old Fräu Schmid had told him she couldn't afford to decorate or buy new tables and chairs. She had joked that a moderate amount of war damage would be nice, if it could be arranged. A friend had told her the compensation was quite generous.

Then he'd been joking, too, when he'd said he would see what he could do. It rather looked as if he actually would be able to arrange something after all.

CHAPTER EIGHTEEN

"Looks like the major's not very happy." Ackerman put his feet up on a table and scuffed them as hard as he could across its polished surface. He'd already wiped them with the tablecloth.

"I don't think he's getting a lot of sense out of them." Dooley cut a thick slice from a sausage and made a sandwich of it between two crackers. "Whoever is running this show appears to be suffering from a nasty case of conflicting objectives."

"Long words for you at this time of day." Burke licked the remains of a slice of cheesecake from his fingers. "At any time of day, come to that."

"Overheard the major say it. Sounded good, I thought."

"So it does, but what's it mean?" Helping himself to another slice, Burke picked cherries from its top before biting into it.

"If you want a free translation, it means that the committee of generals who are bothering the chief of police are adding indecision to incompetence." Carrington paused at the table on his way to the kitchens. "Common sense says locate and contain the enemy. Wait until we've got the strength to tackle them properly."

"Why don't we?" Burke dropped a large blob of cream. He was about to wipe it up, when Ackerman smeared it into the threadbare carpet.

"Because the politicians want the city back to normal as fast as possible."

Not too fast, Ackerman thought. Not until he'd finished

here. He went through into the food preparation area and surreptitiously wrenched an electric socket from the wall.

So far all he'd done was minor acts of vandalism. He'd have to come up with better than that. On her return, doubtless Fräu Schmid would add a few touches of her own, but if she was to get sufficient reparations to redecorate and refurnish, the damage would have to be more than superficial. The more she was able to claim, the bigger his rake-off. He looked about for inspiration.

"Give the men another ten minutes." Revell knew the rest was as much for himself as the others. He took a swig from his bottle of wine. It didn't go well with the food he had eaten.

His conversation on the radio had been frustrating. Even during the course of it, his orders had been modified twice. It was as if plans were being changed from moment to moment, as fresh incidents were reported in and circumstances altered slightly. He could get no information at all as to what other groups might be working on his flanks.

He'd gained the impression that his was the only group hunting down the Russians in the city center. From the sounds of gunfire coming from every point of the compass, he realized that was not the case.

A helicopter passed overhead, but their guard on the door was unable to identify it from the brief glimpse he had. The throbbing beat of its rotors indicated a military type, but that could mean anything, or nothing. It gradually faded from hearing.

Revell looked at his map. Their next objective was on Marienplatz, Munich's main square, the heart of the city. What, he wondered, had decided them on that as their priority target.

103

There were several large public shelters there, as well as subway entrances. That meant a lot of people under dire threat. But a factor that might have weighed as much was the fact that the New Town Hall adjoined it on one side. Either way, with large numbers of civilians in the area, it had all the makings of a messy fight.

Ackerman was alone in the kitchen when the order was passed to move out. Obvious means of creating damage, like causing a gas explosion or turning the fat-fryer up full, he'd had to reject.

Destroying the whole restaurant would be going too far. The only thing he could think of was to leave the doors of the fridges and freezers open.

As he did so, he noticed that a lot of the packs displayed long past use-by dates. That didn't come as any surprise. It tended to bear out the complaints he'd heard from several of the men, about the quality of the food. Most — after tasting such cold dishes as were to be found — had elected instead to dine off brought-in food, such as cheese and sausage.

No wonder the old girl was short of cash. No local would eat there, and most tourists would sample it only the once. He'd be helping the NATO cause if he didn't wreck the place. At least if she went out of business there'd be fewer cases of food poisoning.

As they began to file from the building, Revell heard the return of the helicopter. Its distinctive beat definitely marked it as a gunship, but it still stayed out of sight behind the skyline of buildings.

The noise diminished and he pushed it from his mind. He had counted the last man out of the restaurant, when suddenly the air was filled with its roar. It raced in low across the formal gardens, its downwash throwing the shaped hedges into frantic movement.

He began to run as the beat of the blades and howl of

its engines swamped everything. Behind him the front of the restaurant was blasted apart by a long burst of fire from a 30mm chain gun.

At a speed he hadn't known he could achieve, Revell made it to a subway entrance and threw himself down the steps. He buried himself against an angle of the wall, as he heard the aircraft banking and coming in for another strafing run. But this time it was not the cannon it employed. Instead it rippled a salvo of three rockets.

The first landed short, smashing into the road and gouging a crater that lashed the front of the building with chunks of hard material. Both the second and third missiles plunged straight in through the shattered frontage of the eating place. Their detonations blended and sent jets of dust and debris from every window.

In slow motion, the front wall began to sag. As it folded and fell, so the edge of the roof began to dip, sending a shower of tiles slithering to the road in a clattering hail that went on for a long time.

"That's one of ours." Ackerman vaulted over the edge of the staircase and landed next to the officer. "That was an Apache. What the fuck are they playing at?"

Risking a look, Ackerman was in time to see the upper floors of the restaurant collapsing into the ruins. Then the remainder of the roof caved in, to complete the work of destruction. The place where they'd recently been resting had ceased to exist. Where it had stood, there was only a ragged gap in the row. A thick pall of dust billowed about the street.

Shit. The old girl would never believe he'd had a hand in that. Talk about overdoing it!

Overhead the gunship was still circling, searching for movement on the streets. Against such firepower an attempt to move would be suicidal. Ackerman was thinking that nothing would induce him to go out on that street again, when Revell ordered him to do just that.

"Find the others. Tell them to stay under cover, well dispersed. Let Sgt. Hyde know that I'm going to try the subway. If the civvies got away, then the tunnels will be clear, and we can get to Marienplatz."

Revell watched his messenger get safely to the other side of the road, then had one last go at getting through on the radio. He could get no response from the bunker. It appeared to be off the air completely.

He made his way into the subway. He took no special precautions, didn't expect anybody to be there. By this time in the morning, the evacuation should be well underway, even nearing completion. But if it was, then the effort had not reached this station as yet.

His entrance into the packed ticket hall created an electric reaction. A large part of the crowd cowered fearfully away, trampling each other and crushing some people against the walls and barriers. Another, smaller, section of the mass became aggressive, standing their ground, even edging forward.

A tall blond boy stepped to the front, waving a passport. "I am Swedish. I am a neutral, see, I have—"

Even as he opened the document, he was grabbed and hauled back into the throng. Many of the mob held improvised weapons, and they began to move towards the officer, threateningly.

Broken bottles, lengths of piping, pieces of timber were all displayed as they shouted.

"You'll have to kill us all . . ."

"Come on then . . ."

They were beginning to surround him. Revell tried to fall back towards the entrance. He shouted to them, in English and in German, but they weren't in a mood to listen.

"I'm with the NATO forces—"

"We know your tricks . . ."

"That's how Spetsnaz operate . . ."

Revell sensed that fear was prompting — among some of the civilians — a suicidal last stand against what they thought was a Russian paratrooper.

Rapidly they were becoming more confident as he failed to take positive action. They had managed to surround him and began to close in. Nothing he could say would get through to them, convince them of who he was.

He was the enemy, that was their only thought. The mob rushed at him.

CHAPTER NINETEEN

Revell felt the mass of hands grabbing at him, trying to wrest his submachine gun away from him. A length of timber was swung down at his head. It grazed the side of his helmet and landed hard on his shoulder, numbing his arm. Only the thickness of his padded flak vest prevented it from doing worse harm.

He shouted as loudly as he could, but neither his imperfect German, or English, made any impression on his attackers. Blows rained against his arms and hands where he clung to the MP5. Fingers were plucking at his holster, trying to remove his pistol.

It was the struggling and tussling of the mob itself that prevented their immediate success. Several though had fastened strong grips on his submachine gun, and he could not resist their efforts much longer.

There was a face at the back that Revell recognized. It was Sophia. She was trying to pull the men off, calling to them, but failing to have any effect. Constantly she had to pick herself up after being knocked aside by the mad scramble.

A shot rang out, deafeningly loud in the confined space. The bullet penetrated the suspended ceiling and brought down a light fitting and a shower of fragments of plastic. Still lit, the neon swung back and forth, making wild shadow patterns on faces.

Two more shots rang out and destroyed other panels and neons above them before the crowd finally backed off. The shouting and baying halted, and Sophia took advantage of the lull to tell everyone she could reach that she knew Revell.

Andrea had her MP5 levelled at the attackers, who were now slowly pressing back into the main body of the crowd. Apart from them a little, stood a police officer, not knowing which side to join.

Crossing to Revell, Sophia looked as if she would have put her arms about him, but she saw Andrea's expression and stopped short in front of him.

"I am sorry. We are all frightened. There have been shots at some who tried to leave, to see what was happening. We thought the Russians had taken the city."

"Well, they haven't, not all of it. Are things bad down here?"

"It is getting worse. There have been fights. There is talk that one man was killed on the platform, and that others were wounded by knives and bottles. How much longer shall we be down here?"

He could hear the strain in Sophia's voice. For the first time he was conscious of being able to hear a constant undercurrent of groaning and crying coming from the crowd. Occasionally there would be an aggressive demand for silence, followed by a loud slap and then more shouting from several voices, accompanied by ever louder wailing.

"I understood they were going to get you all out through the subway system. Has nothing been done?"

"A few have been seen to go into the tunnels. Most are too frightened to make the attempt. I believe it is far worse down there. They have no sanitation for such numbers."

"I'll see if I can find out what's supposed to be happening. As I understood it, everything was organized."

Accompanied by both women, Revell went to the entrance and a few steps up towards street level, to get better radio reception. Though he tried for several minutes, he had no better luck than earlier.

His men wouldn't like it, but they could cope with being hunted by one of their own gunships, until the situation was brought under control somehow. But the civilians below needed reassurance. There was none he could give them. It wasn't even wise to mention the evacuation plan, in case it had been dropped. A false hope could be as dangerous as a real fear in these conditions.

"Does no one care? They can have no idea what conditions are like in the shelters." Sophia was near to tears.

"I expect everything is being thrown in to the effort to clear the Russians out first." Revell could think of no other excuse to make. "It's unpleasant I know, but they are safe."

In truth though, that wasn't something that Revell could be certain of at all. He thought again of those senior officers he'd seen in the bunker. There might be those among them who were brilliant at organizing logistics — the nuts and bolts of running and feeding an army — but this was a situation they were hardly equipped to handle.

The comfort of the air-conditioned bunker, with its generous allocation of space, gave them no insight into what it was actually like for the other half million in the city. Very likely they had not even given it a thought, taking it for granted that the conditions that prevailed for them were universal.

The general's bunker had been built long before the war. Originally it had been solely intended for use as a civil defence operations center, in a post nuclear strike scenario.

Shelters built at the start of the war, for the mass of the population, had few of the same refinements. Civilian administrations had balked at the high expenditure involved in fitting all of them out to that standard. In the majority of cases, air-filtration, sanitation, and the necessary stocks of food and medical supplies had been given scant attention.

The rapid advances of the first Russian attack on West Germany had triggered a defeatist attitude among many

110

politicians. Many had even tried to convince themselves that occupation was for the best. In their eyes, it would at least result in reunification.

But the stalling and then staying of the onslaught, resulted in the formation of the huge north-south no-man's-land — the Zone. With the armies locked in battle within that well-defined area, those who opposed the shelter program had been able to get it cut back. What was happening in Munich was the consequence of that.

Ripper vaulted down into the stairwell.

"Major, we've spotted a squad of Reds trying to hot-wire a truck. Think it could be the ones who shot their own buddies?"

"How many of them are there?"

"Five. Sgt. Hyde has gone after them. He's taken four men and the machine gun."

Even as Ripper spoke, from a block away came a rattle of automatic fire, punctuated by several grenade explosions.

CHAPTER TWENTY

Andrea had been deliberately edging closer to Sophia, realizing that her proximity made the girl uncomfortable. She tried to see what Revell had seen in her.

Attractive, in a soft well-manicured way, but the makeup applied hours before did nothing for her now. Lack of sleep, stress, and the conditions below had smudged or removed most of it. Her clothes, too, Andrea noted, were soiled and crumpled. Yet still, she sensed, the major was attracted to her.

Having reduced the girl to a shivering bundle of nerves, Andrea moved away and contented herself with staring at her, while toying with her submachine gun.

They moved up to the street when they heard Hyde returning. Sophia hung back at the top of the stairs.

"Four down." Hyde was pushing a Russian ahead of him. "This one tried playing dead, until Scully kicked him in the balls."

"We'll drop him off at the command bunker on the way. If they've got their act together, they'll be able to carry out some sort of interrogation. I doubt they'll get much though."

If the Russian had understood, as was likely, Revell gave him credit for not showing it. His face wore a sullen frown, and he looked out at his captors from under bushy eyebrows as he kept his head bowed.

Scully produced an antitank rocket launcher. "They had this. I suppose other groups will have them as well."

"More than likely." Revell examined the weapon. A bullet

112

had smashed the trigger group, rendering it useless. "Did they have anything else of interest?"

"Only these." Hyde displayed a pack of demolition charges and small antipersonnel mines. "No papers of any description."

"We'll hang on to the ordnance." Listening for the gunship, Revell thought he could detect the faint and distant beat of its rotors, but couldn't be certain. "Best we move out to our next objective, before that maniac does another sweep over this quarter."

Even as he said it, the chopper lifted over the buildings at the far side of the formal gardens and its roar burst upon them.

There was no chance to dive into cover. As the machine swooped closer, Revell could only throw himself down in the road. Before he cradled his head in his arms, he had a clear view of the stubby barrel of the chain gun mounted below the craft's fuselage and of the half-empty rocket pods on its stub wings. A salvo pulverized cars on the other side of the road.

Their prisoner grabbed his chance, tugging himself away from Sgt. Hyde, who tried to pull him to the ground. He looked around once, and then bolted for the entrance to the subway.

Hyde could only shield his eyes against the storm of dust thrown up as the gunship passed very low overhead. From somewhere he heard a shout that carried even above the noise of flailing blades and screaming twin engines.

As the blast of sound diminished, it was replaced by another. The first shout was joined by others that blended with it to create a banshee howl. Above that rose a scream of agony that transcended any Hyde had ever heard.

It went higher and higher, reaching a note it did not seem possible for a human voice to attain and hold. For a moment it dropped to a racking sob, then soared once more, to end abruptly and be replaced once more by the howl.

With Revell, the sergeant raced for the steps. When they reached the bottom it took a moment for their eyes to adjust to the gloom. Before them a tightly packed crowd backed away in a semicircle from a bundle of rags on the floor.

The bundle moved spastically, ugly slithering sounds coming from it. Bending closer, hesitating before he reached out, Hyde turned the bundle over.

Tearing fingernails had clawed the Russian's face until there was nothing left beyond scraps of ragged flesh adhering to cheek and jawbones. Everything else was gone. Close to the still moving man lay an arm, pulled off in a frenzied tug-of-war as he was fought over. The remaining limbs were resting at odd angles to the victim, all were clearly broken. Ends of bone grated together as the Spetsnaz soldier writhed.

Taking out his pistol, Hyde held it close to the Russian's head and pulled the trigger. A final convulsive spasm shook the Russian as fragments of skull and spongy brain matter flew across the floor, and then it was over.

"Let's get out of here." Revell was all too well aware that he had come perilously close to meeting a similar fate in that place.

As he backed out, the mob edged forward to once more engulf the body. Neither Revell or Hyde looked back to see what they were doing with it.

The same priest was at the door when Revell left Sophia at the Theatiner Church. He had looked out at the men with the major, seen their tired, dirt-streaked faces, the blood on their battle dress and weapons.

Without having to ask, he knew that his prayers had

been in vain. Before closing the door, he watched them go. All his life he had been a pacifist, now as he turned back into the church he discovered a doubt in his mind. He looked at the many young men in the pews. Most were foreign laborers, brought in to maintain production at the many armorment factories; others were tourists. But there were a number, a larger number than he might have expected — who were German.

There had been a time when he had admired the courage, as he had thought of it, of those who had dared to say that they would not fight. Now he was reconsidering his attitude. Pacifism had always been a cornerstone of his belief.

Where was the courage in letting others give their lives for you? At worst, those young men had to put up with scorn and insults. That might take away their dignity, their self-esteem at times, but it let them keep their lives.

Making his way to the altar once more, the priest found a quiet corner and went down on his knees, bowing his head low.

His prayer was an inward thing, the words being framed but not uttered by his lips. Before, he had prayed that the major would not have to kill. This time, the priest added the supplication that he should have the strength not to condemn the officer if he had to.

As they passed the New Town Hall on the way to their objective, Revell had half-expected to come under fire from the bunker entrance. To ward off the possibility, he tried repeatedly to get through on the radio as they approached. Still he could get nothing.

Overhead a second gunship had joined the first. They beat back and forth across the city. Sometimes they would dive out of sight, then there would come the sound of rocket and cannon fire. Shortly after came the multiple, devastating impacts.

"Looks like they're attacking targets of opportunity." Hyde listened to another long burst of cannon fire. "They can't be under any sort of ground control. They're treating Munich like a free-fire zone."

"I'd like to know why." Revell took a swig from a can of lemonade. "From the shooting we can hear, I'd say there must be other hunting teams engaging the Russians around here. At this rate, how long is it going to be before we bump into one, and get involved in a shoot-out with our own side?"

CHAPTER TWENTY-ONE

The door to the bunker was almost off its hinges, partially concealing a body; and from what Revell could see of its condition, a grenade had done the damage.

Just inside were three more dead and the mangled remains of a machine gun. Sections of splintered furniture were scattered about. Smoke from their smoldering edges bit into his throat and made his eyes water.

"No bodies outside." Hyde stepped over a large puddle of blood. "How the hell could the Reds have got close enough to use grenades without getting casualties?"

Carrington entered behind them, paused, and ran his hand over the back of the door. "Major, that grenade went off right inside. All the gouge marks are in the back of the timber. If it had been thrown from the street, how did it do *that?*"

"Spetsnaz often use NATO uniforms." Looking at the scorch marks on the walls and ceiling, Hyde knew the corporal was correct. The door must have been almost closed when the explosion occurred. "Maybe they tricked their way inside?"

"Not very likely." Revell recalled his own reception by the guards. "The mood these men were in, it was definitely shoot first and ask questions later.

"The alternative is that they got in through the main building, and came out this way. That doesn't look good."

Submachine gun at the ready, Revell started down the stairs. The lights were still on, but the air-conditioning was not. Dust and smoke hung in the air. There was a strong smell of cordite, and other less easily identified odors.

In the corridor the sentry lay dead. He had been killed by a single shot through the head. The arrangement of his body and the position of the wound suggested he had been turning to see who was coming through the double doors behind him.

They were half-open. As Revell stepped through, he knew what he was going to find. Each room contained its quota of dead. The Russians had worked systematically through the bunker.

"Must have used silencers." Hyde pulled bodies aside to check if any of those at the bottom still lived. "Got in, killed the staff, opened the door, got the sentry before he could give the alarm and then bombed the door guard. By that time it didn't matter what noise they made. There was no one left to hear."

In the communication room Revell found every piece of equipment smashed. In confirmation of their reconstruction, they also found a dead Russian paratrooper. When they turned him over, they discovered his silenced pistol underneath.

A police officer had managed to unholster his own gun and use it to good effect. The weapon was still grasped in his hand.

All of the officers were dead. Among them was Col. Klee. Right at the end he had tried to redeem himself. His body shielded that of one of the women telephone operators. It had been a sadly futile gesture. Bullets had passed through his thin frame and killed her also.

Whirling around as he heard a noise behind him, Hyde's finger tightened over his trigger. The sound came from a small side room. He went through. It was coming from within a storage cupboard, tucked away at the end of a row of lockers.

A body obstructed the door. He pulled it away and, covered by the major, snatched it open.

"We could hear you moving. You'd never be any good at hide and seek." Hyde immediately regretted his flippancy.

Gebert collapsed into Revell's arms. Sweat poured down his face, soaking his collar. His pants were wet to the knee from another source. "We thought they had come back. I had cramp, I could not help it."

Aware for the first time that he had wet himself, Gebert

tried to cover the large damp patches with a bloodstained folder.

From out of the cupboard behind him came Stadler. The chief of police looked grim, despite having to blink and shield his eyes against the unaccustomed glare. "Did they get everyone?"

"Looks as if they weren't in a mood for taking prisoners. How did they get in?" Revell assisted the mayor to a chair.

"From upstairs." Gebert fanned himself with the folder, then recalled what it had covered and put it on his lap. "They must have known the layout precisely. Those damned agents again. There can be nothing about this city that the enemy does not know."

"They didn't know about your cupboard."

Despite what he had been through, Gebert smiled. It faded as swiftly as it appeared, when he noticed the body that had been pulled aside. "I suppose when they caught him in here, they assumed no one else was hiding."

Stadler had brushed himself and straightened his tie. He pushed his hair back into place. "There is now absolutely no control over what is happening in the city, besides any that might have been established at a purely local level. We've got to regain overall control. Do your men still hold the police headquarters?"

"I presume so. With a couple of platoons and that armory, it would take more than a plane load of Russians to retake it."

"Then we must transfer there, Major. As quickly as possible."

They left the way they had entered, slipping and sliding on the partially congealed mess on the door. The air outside tasted better, but carried the stench of smoke from burning vehicles.

"My poor city. Poor Munich." Gebert forgot his own discomfort as he saw several dark columns rising high over the rooftops. "The Russian barbarians are destroying it, piece by piece."

Stadler noticed several dead civilians on the road. "And its people, but they are doing that at a much faster rate."

It was only a few hundred meters to police headquarters. The journey took them forty-five minutes. Cutting the corner of Marienplatz, they came under fire from a sniper post on the top floor of a bank.

From the scattering of huddled forms, it was clear the gunman had been active for a while.

Some civilians, caught in the open, had been pinned down. They cowered behind flower tubs and benches, too terrified to move.

Revell saw a woman, driven by desperation, make a break from behind a pot of shrubs towards a side street. She had gone perhaps ten steps when the first shot caught her and she stumbled. Dragging her right leg, she tried to go on, but a second bullet passed through her body. Collapsing silently, she lay still.

Dooley looked to the major for permission, before unslinging the last of their rocket launchers. He sighted carefully before firing.

The missile soared the short distance to the target in a dead-straight trajectory. As Dooley had intended, the high-explosive warhead impacted immediately below the window from which the sniper was operating.

Intended to withstand the armor of main battle tanks, the fabric of the building presented no impediment to the jet of molten material projected into the room.

Every window was blasted out by the pressure generated, as blast and flame flattened thin partition walls and roared through the top floor of the bank.

When they moved on once more, they attracted no more sniper fire.

CHAPTER TWENTY-TWO

"Was Col. Klee among the dead in the bunker?" Stadler took off a headset and rubbed his ears with the palms of his hands.

"Yes, he was." Revell had to think for a moment. "In the circumstances, it's for the best. His life would have been very unpleasant when all this was over. Why do you want to know now?"

"Because if he wasn't, I'd just made up my mind to kick him in the balls. Several times. Very hard."

The commissioner looked at the handful of officers working in the communications room. Less than a third of the positions were filled, and those by inexperienced operators. "The men I detailed to accompany his column from the barracks tell me that they're still there, and not likely to move in the foreseeable future. I've men being killed and others working themselves into nervous breakdowns, and *they* won't move without an order in writing."

"What about those gunships? Have you been able to do anything about them?" As he spoke Revell could hear the distant stutter of the chain-guns engaging.

"I managed to get through to air-traffic control. They're trying to contact them. I'm hoping it'll be soon."

"What about the shooting in the center?"

"It seems that groups of my men formed themselves into impromptu SWAT teams. It appears they are having some success, but they need ammunition and reinforcement to maintain the pressure."

"You've riot vehicles parked below." Revell recalled the

transport that had sheltered them during the earlier assault on the HQ. "Put a squad in each. Knock out the windows and pad the sides with loads of spare body armor, and there you are, improvised APCs."

"Good." Stadler got through to the armory on the internal phone. "We'll use police drivers. They will know all the back roads."

"If they *do* draw fire, it'll enable us to locate others of the Russian squads." Through the window Revell could see several pillars of smoke rising in the early afternoon air. He waited until the commissioner had finished on the phone.

"I think those fires are spreading. What's the position with the fire service?"

"That I would like to know, Major. Not long after I went to the bunker, every unit and crew was ordered out of the city. The instruction came from the highest level in their service. I need hardly add that we can not trace Herr Friedmann, who issued it. It is my hope that we shall be able to eventually. Also he lied about summoning help from outside Munich."

"Can't you get them back?" In the street below, Revell saw that the trees were swaying in a breeze sufficiently strong to shake a continual rain of leaves. Cinders and sparks were landing with them, and smoldering.

"Some I have been able to recall. Also machines that sabotage had put out of action are now mobile again. We can deploy those to contain the situation. For once the cleverness of the enemy agents has rebounded on them."

Mayor Gebert bustled into the room. "Sorry, Karl. What a time to get the shits. How are we doing?" He scanned the screens, making little sense of them.

"Not as bad as we might be. I established contact with the outlying police station. They have men standing by to come in as we call for them. Army territorial units can't help much. They've been reduced to cadre level by recent drafts. I hadn't realized just how bad the manpower and equipment situation

122

was after that last call up of reservists and the combing out of depot staffs."

"The column from the airport?" Gebert picked up a sandwich from a stack on a side table, opened it up for a look inside, pulled a face, and put it back.

"Still stalled three kilometers from the center. Looks like the Reds anticipated such a move and established roadblocks. The column has lost some armor, but they're looking for a way round."

"Tell them not to lose contact altogether with the Russian groups. Have them leave a token force to keep them busy."

Stadler exchanged glances with Revell. "The major has already suggested that."

"Yes, yes, of course you would. Sorry, Major, must learn to leave military matters to the military. Great, isn't it? Here I am, holding the position I've always dreamed of, and when it comes to a situation like this, I'm as useful as a tit on a nun." An agonized look crossed Gebert's face. "Oh Christ, I've got to go again. You know where I'll be if you need me."

"As the mayor has so much, eh, on his mind," Stadler waited until he was out of hearing, "there is something else you should know, Major."

"I figured things were sounding too good all of a sudden. So what's the problem?"

Stadler punched up a display. "Here you see all the locations where my men are engaging the Russians, but there is one firefight in which none of my men are involved."

"A group of officers who've lost contact? Maybe they've no radio."

"I cannot believe that several sets would malfunction at the same time. Impossible. The volume of gunfire reported is considerable. Too much for my men to get close enough to determine what is happening."

"Then we're getting help we didn't ask for."

"That's the trouble. We did ask for it, or rather Col. Klee

asked for it." Stadler threw a notebook across the room. "I don't know who they are, or how they got here, but I suspect that the garrison commander's invitation to a free-for-all has been accepted."

"And your men are unable to determine who's involved?" Revell wondered how hard they had tried, in the face of heavy fire.

"I know what you think. Two were wounded while trying. I feel like I am sitting on a powder keg." Stadler blanked the screen. "A measure of control has been restored, but there are still half a million civilians trapped in the shelters. There is one right under this private battle. It holds over a thousand. If they should flood onto the streets . . ."

"The Russians would use the opportunity to shift position in the confusion. That's what they're like. They'd certainly not hesitate to use the crowd as human shields." That was a tactic Warpac troops had grown skilled at using. Revell had often seen them employ it in battles in the Zone. They would advance, driving a wall of refugees before them, and frequently they had deliberately situated supply bases and static units in among the scattered settlements.*

"I also believe they would do that. For many of the civilians, their breaking point must be close. It will not take much to generate mass hysteria in a crowded shelter. They will run out onto the street like so many lemmings. Others will hear what is happening, and there will be a chain reaction."

"It'll result in a bloodbath." It needed no great feat of imagination on Revell's part to picture what such an event would be like. The blind stampede and its accompanying frenzy would kill and maim thousands, many more than the Russian bullets.

Even with the infiltrators eliminated, the result would be a

*ZONE ONE HARD TARGET.

mass exodus from the city and the total dislocation of vital war work. Demoralization on such a scale could even bring the West Germans to sue for a separate peace, when its inevitable domino effect had rippled through the whole country.

Stadler felt very tired, and knew he looked it. In the run up to the OcktoberFest, he had been working eighteen hours a day. Like the city as a whole he had been looking forward to the beer festival as an outlet, a chance to unwind. Instead, this had happened.

"Major Revell. I will do anything to save this city from the fate the Russians are trying to bring about. I will not see it ruined or its people slaughtered through enemy action, or through their own panic. We must bring matters under control. We must do it very quickly."

"I'll take my best men and find out what's happening."

Stadler made ready to put on his headset again. "While my men cannot get near that fighting, it is not possible to reassure the civilians in the nearby shelters. If the only way you can stop the battles is to fire on our own side, then don't hesitate to do it."

"It won't come to that, I hope." Already it had crossed Revell's mind that it might, but that would be a last resort.

The police chief wanted control of the army and police forces in the city. To give him that, Revell and his men might first have to unleash a lot of controlled violence.

CHAPTER TWENTY-THREE

Vehicles parked in the narrow street were riddled with bullet holes. Several sat low on the ground, or at odd angles, their tires shot to ribbons.

For the first time in the city, they had seen tracer employed. A long stream of it had poured from a window in a department store and into a drugstore opposite. Some had missed the mark. Striking the stone wall, they had flown off at wild angles to cause more random damage.

"It's like something out of a fucking western." From a safe distance, Scully watched the exchanges of fire. "Pity there isn't a sheriff who can come galloping into town and clean it all up."

"No sheriff. Just us, with you as Deputy Dog."

Sgt. Hyde fingered a long tear across the shoulder of his flak jacket. His ribs still ached where another stray bullet— most of its energy spent—had thumped into him.

They had learnt little from their reconnaissance, except that both buildings were well defended and impossible to approach. He and the major had seen no sign of the men holding out. Attempts to establish contact from a distance had been hopeless, only bringing fire down on them.

Now, with Scully and Andrea, Hyde waited to give covering fire while the drugstore was rushed. The seconds ticked away on his watch. The butt and barrel of the grenade launcher had warmed in his hands. The unit had worked their way as close as possible to the rear of the building. Sheltering in the angle of a wall close behind them was the assault party, led by the major.

Andrea would fire first. Her high-explosive round would blast down the back door, then the three of them would put batton rounds into the opening as fast as they could. Right until the instant the squad reached it.

The 40mm grenade soared the fifty meters to the target and scored a direct hit. There was a roar of noise from the detonation that blended with the crash of falling brickwork and splintering wood. Loading and firing as fast as they could, the three concentrated their aim on the smoke-wreathed opening.

A burst of light machinegun fire from an upper floor made spurts of dust beside the running group, then ceased as blunt-nosed plastic slugs shattered the remaining glass and tore into the room.

Revell leapt the fallen remains of the scorched and splintered door. At the far end of the passageway beyond a figure knelt on its knees, clutching its face.

"What unit?" There was not the time for gentle methods. Revell jabbed the barrel of his submachine gun into the side of the man's neck. "Who are you with?"

"You're fucking NATO."

"Too bloody true." Revell didn't remove the submachine gun. "Who are you, what unit?"

"Two hundred ninety first Infantry. Our captain heard there was a flap on and sent us in to have a scout round, see the position before he brought the rest of the company. Only we got ambushed, and had our radio knocked out. We dived in here and have been trading shots for the last hour."

"How many of you are there?" Revell handed the man a field dressing to apply to a wound on his cheek.

"We lost a couple, including our sergeant, when we got hit. Only five of us left, I think."

"Okay, you go on up ahead of us." Revell helped the soldier to his feet. "Make sure they know who's coming. From what I have seen and can hear, there's a lot of trigger-happy people about."

Every inch of floor was smothered in spilt pills and broken medicine bottles. They crunched underfoot. Cases of ointment and syrups had been punctured. Their pungent, sticky contents oozed through the rows of holes in their cartons and dripped from shelf to shelf, then to the floor. The same mess was on the stairs, Tablets beneath their tread, acting like ball bearings, made every step difficult.

When they reached the upper floor, they found only two men still on their feet. Or rather, on their hands and knees. They were searching through scattered magazines for ammunition. A third soldier lay unconscious with a bad head wound. The fourth was dead. He had taken several bullets in the throat.

As if at a signal, the firing from across the road had ceased. Using a fragment of broken mirror like a periscope, Revell examined the department store.

"Whoever they are, I think they've skipped." Using the view in the reflection, he made another survey before radioing in his findings. He stayed low, waiting until they were away from the front of the building before standing. "We'll have to check it out though."

"What about us?" His face swathed in bandages, the infantryman found it hard to speak.

"You can't move that head wound case, and you're not in any state for fighting. Better if the four of you hang on here, until an ambulance can get through. There's a police team following us, they'll take care of things. Sit tight, you've done all you can."

"Yeah, but who have we been fighting?" His face becoming swollen, the infantryman was hardly able to articulate.

"If *you* don't know, then sure as hell *I* don't."

As they left the building, Revell waved on a squad of police who were cautiously approaching. From a slow, painstaking pace, hugging a wall in single file, bent almost double, they immediately straightened up and began to bunch as they walked at a normal speed.

A spent bullet cracking a window nearby restored them quickly to their former caution.

Revell led the squad a good way up the road before they broke in through the rear of a building and, with extreme caution, out through its front.

Crossing the road drew no fire, and they began to edge towards the department store. At the far end of the street, safely out of any likely line of fire, several more police stood anxiously waiting for the moment when they could dash to the entrance of the shelter.

As they passed its dark opening, Revell could hear crying and swearing from below, and what he thought might be a sharp smack. That was followed by violent shouting, and the sounds of what could be a fight. Two bodies lay just outside the entrance. That of an elderly man bore no trace of a wound. Beside his was that of a young woman. Her wrists had been slashed and her flesh had a pallid hue. Both looked as if they had been pushed out.

"Suicide and heart attack case most likely."

Hyde had also heard the noises. "Can't blame them for chucking these two out. Bad enough down there without sharing the accommodations with the dead."

The smell of oil and gasoline was strong in the street. Most of the vehicles' fuel tanks had been punctured, and the gutters ran with the mixture.

"One tracer in this lot and the whole road would have gone up." Dooley had come forward at the major's beckoning.

"The front door is still in one piece." Revell had had a quick look at the store's entrance. Set slightly back from the sidewalk, it had survived the blitz of bullets. "If we use a grenade, we might ignite this mess. Reckon you can take it out with a shoulder charge?"

"I'll give it a try. Need a bit of a run up though, Major." With slow deliberation, Dooley paced out his run, turned, and charged.

His collision with the stout teak frames made all the plate glass windows vibrate. The glass in the doors didn't break, but the double lock couldn't survive the impact, and the doors burst open inwards.

Dooley tumbled headlong into the store, rolling into painful contact with a counter. A shower of lipsticks and other cosmetics came down on top of him. By the time he'd brushed them aside, the others had already dived in past him.

It was too huge a place for them to search really thoroughly, but by the time they returned to the ground floor, they could be fairly certain that none of the mysterious machine gunners remained.

On the third floor they found heaps of empty cartridge cases and evidence of blood. There was more on a stairway, and by an open fire exit out onto a loading bay.

"So what do we do, Sarge." Dooley nursed his sore shoulder. "Track them down?"

"As we don't have a red Indian tracker in the section, I don't really think that's a starter, do you?"

Dooley shrugged, wincing as it aggravated his soreness. "I suppose we just wait for them to surface, and then we go haring off after them again."

"Something like that."

Revell returned with Andrea and Scully from a search of the rear service road. "They're long gone. It's like a rabbit warren out there. They could be virtually next door or on the other side of the city by this time. We'll go back the front way, let the police know its all clear to contact the civies in the shelter."

They had reached the front door and were about to pass through it, when there was the report of a muted explosion. A ripple of fire streaked beneath the parked traffic.

An instant later a wall of red and yellow flame rose in front of them and black smoke billowed into the store.

CHAPTER TWENTY-FOUR

A ferocious heat struck the walls of glass flanking the entrance, and there was a sharp crack as one wall split with the sudden dramatic expansion.

Tires quickly fuelled the blaze, and then the plastic and cloth of the vehicle interiors. Another window snapped from top to bottom, and then fell apart. The window displays began to smoulder and crisp.

"Hope the fire brigade get here quick." Scully lifted a hand to shield his face from the waves of roasting air. "They could lose the whole street."

"Dooley, look about for fire hoses."

"Aw, come on, Major. Let's leave it to the experts."

Even as he complained, Dooley saw a blackened figure lurch past the door, collapse, and burst into flame.

"The shelter . . ."

Revell needed to add nothing more. It took several long minutes to locate a fire hose, another to unreel it and run it to the door. The first precious moments after the water surged through had to be used in spraying the burning window, before they could move forward to tackle the heart of the fire.

"Which is best?" Dooley had to grip the nozzle hard as the surging pressure of the water threatened to buck it from his hands. "Do I use jet or spray?"

"The jet." Even behind the shield offered by the cascade, Revell could still feel his face scorching. "It'll reach further."

The windshields of the nearest vehicles exploded into millions of fragments as they were suddenly quenched by the stream. Masses of steam rose from interiors and panels as the water hit them, but still flames flared to the height of the first-floor windows.

Paint was blistering and shrinking to expose bare wood on doors, as lead was beginning to drip from downspouts. Every time the direction of the jet was switched to flush the burning fuel from under the vehicles, it was almost simultaneously replenished by that still running from the punctured fuel tanks. Reignition followed immediately.

Another civilian, head covered by a jacket, made a run from the air-raid shelter. A gas tank in an Opel ruptured beside him, and he was hidden in the resulting explosion. It lifted as a great red flaring tongue of flame, to reveal a smoldering body hurled against a street sign and draped around it like a perfectly tossed horseshoe.

Others jammed the shelter entrance. Revell could sometimes glimpse them through the thick smoke. They would edge forward a shuffling half step, then be driven back by a fresh outbreak. Two fell forward across the sidewalk. No one attempted to pull them back and they began to burn. A further tank explosion close to them hid the scene from sight behind impenetrable flame and smoke.

"Get up to the next floor, find another hose up there." As fast as they subdued the fire aboard one vehicle, it would break out afresh as they switched the jet to another. Revell could hear screams now, very clearly, above the roar of flame and the constant banging of bursting tires. Showers of fiery rubber droplets carpeted the sidewalk and started outbreaks in litter bins and among the bubbling paintwork of the storefronts.

From above, a second hose added its efforts, and under the combined drenching the flames began to recede, until it licked only from the interior of vehicles whose glass had resisted the jets.

There was no help that could be given to the victims who had fallen in the street. The two bodies they had seen earlier were charred beyond recognition and no longer human in appearance.

The shelter entrance was deeply layered with black soot that was greasy to the touch. A few steps down the lighting still functioned, but the globes over the bulbs were similarly coated and gave no light until Revell dragged his hand across them and removed some of the residue.

As he went deeper, the air became roastingly hot and foul with the trapped stench of the smoke. It looked as if the shelter had once been the basement area of the store. With benches fitted and an exit made to the street, it was obviously intended to serve both shoppers and pedestrians alike.

This time it had served no one. Huddled together at the foot of the stairs, in corners, even on and beneath the benches, were hundreds and hundreds of people.

None of them moved. Smothered in yet more of the soot, they were like dark apparitions. At points in the otherwise blank walls — where heavily barred doors presumably led to the store — were heaps of bodies. Here alone the universal covering of adhering black particles had been disturbed.

Where hands had scrabbled and torn at the strong metal, masses of finger marks exposed the paint beneath. The desperation of those frenzied efforts was illustrated by the many daubs and streaks of blood.

Andrea had followed the major inside. She looked around at the row upon row of dead. Many were still in the evening clothes they were wearing when the air raid sirens had sounded in the small hours.

"The fires sucked all the air out, replaced it with this." Running his fingers along the top of a ledge, Revell rubbed the residue between his fingertips.

"They had no other way out?" Andrea stepped over a corpse, that of a young girl in an expensive leather coat. She avoided contact with any surface.

"Apparently not. Another result of the cuts in the civil defence program, when Gorbechev's PR men spouted off about more Soviet cuts."

"And still there are so many in the West who believe in socialism and communism. None of this would have been possible, if they had not had so many traitors to help them."

"Maybe we'll get lucky, and run into a few of them." Revell turned his back on the masses of dead and went out.

For a little longer, Andrea stayed, not seeing the bodies, not smelling the tainted air. In a corner of her mind, in a section of her memory that might have been labelled vengeance in anyone else, she was storing the event away. In her case though, what had happened here brought no thought of revenge. It was just another reason for hating.

From the direction of the river came the loud punching thumps of cannon fire. The airport column. They had reached the Maximilian Bridge and were engaging Soviet troops on the west bank. Detached columns were crossing to the north and south. Soon they would either get behind the enemy, or force them to fall back.

That was what Revell was hoping for. He was waiting. It had been a mad race to get into position. An aggravating delay had been caused by their difficulty in breaking into the furniture store he had picked as an ideal site for the ambush. Eventually they had resorted to using an abandoned Rolls-Royce as a battering ram. The heavy bronze doors of the up-market establishment had not been able to withstand that sort of treatment.

From their vantage point, they could see the length of the wide Maximilianstrasse in either direction, and long sweeps of the ring road that formed the other arms of the intersection.

Ripper laid three spare magazines on the polished top of the writing desk he was using as a rest. "Think that'll be enough?"

Having laid out six of the thirty-round clips at his fire position, Dooley looked across and shook his head. "We've got it, we might as well use it. When we get back in the Zone, it'll be a case of counting every last bullet, and making it count. I'm enjoying not having to worry on that score."

"What the hell is that vandal doing?" Garrett had been watching Carrington pull down drapes and flimsy partitions between room displays in the upstairs showroom.

"Maybe they offend his sense of taste." Sgt. Hyde looked pointedly at the pair of rocket launchers beside Dooley. "Or maybe he doesn't want the backwash from those to start a fire. You should have thought of that. I know you're tired, so am I, but that's no reason to get sloppy. Give the corporal a hand."

Through his binoculars, Revell could see activity on the bridge. Although it was partially obscured by the overhead trolley car power lines, he could make out the hull shape of a big eight-wheeled Luch armored car.

Moments after he saw the stab of flame from its cannon muzzle, he heard the savage crack of its firing. Another drew up alongside and added its firepower.

It wouldn't be long. The Russians wouldn't be able to withstand that sort of pressure for any length of time. And when they fell back, it would be to run right into his sights.

CHAPTER TWENTY-FIVE

Edging forward in turns, the armored cars continued to blast away with their main and secondary armorments at an unseen target. Most of their stray shots were soaked up by the trees that flanked the long avenue, but some skimmed over the broad surface of the road to destruction elsewhere.

Chunks of stone and scabs of metal were punched from the big monument in the middle of the road, as high explosive and armor-piercing rounds struck it. Other cannon shells self-destructed against parked trolley cars and street signs.

From unseen sources behind the massive eight-wheelers came a storm of small-arms fire. Through his glasses, Revell could see bark flying from trees under the combined impacts, and stationary cars shuddering and bouncing on their suspension, due to the same cause.

"They'll have to back away from that lot." Sighting on the last of the long line of trees, Dooley waited for his targets to come into view. "Here, you don't think they'll slug it out to the finish with those wagons, do you?"

"I imagine their orders are to create the maximum disruption to the life of the city." Revell had already considered and dismissed the possibility. "When things get too hot, they'll move on and make a nuisance of themselves elsewhere."

"Looks like you're right, Major." For a brief moment, Hyde thought he saw a figure moving among the trees.

"I've got him as well." Ripper confirmed the sergeant's sighting. "About ten trees up on the left-hand side. Heading straight towards us."

Revell examined the area pinpointed, but saw nothing.

136

"Just the one?"

"Just the one. Don't know if it's the same one though." Ripper eased the safety off his MP5. "It's a mite far, but you want me to see if I can stir anything up?"

"No, hold your fire. They'll be more than one. We want them all in the open."

Switching his attention back to the armored cars, Revell saw that they had started to move forward cautiously. There were short nervous bursts of fire from their coaxial machine guns as they came on.

"They've lost sight of the Russians. They're just playing safe." Coming along behind the armored cars, Revell could see a dozen men on foot, hugging close to the big hulls for cover. Much further back a larger body of men was fanning out to take advantage of the cover offered by the trees.

"Shouldn't be long." Before him, Hyde took in the wide expanse of the intersection. From above, its surface was confused with a wild, seemingly illogical pattern of road markings that made his eyes go funny as he looked at them. "I've got them. Corner of the building opposite, the fur shop."

"Not yet. I'll say when." Revell had seen the two Russians. His caution was warranted. A moment later three more appeared on the other side of the carriageway, at the end of the line of trees.

Their targets were at the extreme effective range of their weapons. Revell was having to take the gamble that the enemy would elect to come straight on, across the intersection. If they chose instead to break into a building and mousehole further along the block, then his men would not get another chance. That was the choice, fire now in the certainty that some would get away, or gamble that they would maintain their straight line retreat. Being wrong would mean they'd all get away.

Through his binoculars he watched them, trying to read their intentions. They were all together now, partially hidden by an angle of the wall. Gestures and movement within the group seemed to suggest that there were two options being heatedly debated. Strange that at such a time they should employ democracy, when they were far more used to dictatorship.

The decision they came to was acted on immediately. With the nearest of the armored cars only a couple of hundred meters off, they broke from their partial cover and sprinted into the road.

Tracking them, Revell had already decided on the point at which he'd order his men to fire. He was about to, when the chance was taken from him.

Out of the large ground-floor windows of an imposing building on the other side of the crossroads, someone spurted several streams of tracer.

One struck short and began to skip towards the runners, scattering lethal ricochets before it. Three more found their targets immediately.

Taken in the flank, the only Russian to get time to turn and level his AK47 never got off a shot. He fell riddled with bullets, across his companions.

"Who the fuck did that?" Dooley still sighted on the center of the crossroads, finger on the trigger.

Saying nothing, Revell observed the armored cars drive forward until they drew up twenty meters from the bodies. A turret hatch opened cautiously and a commander looked out. His companion in the other vehicle followed suit, and the two of them looked uncomprehendingly at the corpses.

"Are we going down, Major?" Hyde gathered up the magazines he had laid out, and returned them to his pouches.

"Well, we're doing no damned good up here. Have the men shoulder their weapons. I've no wish to get smeared by a trigger-happy turret-gunner by mistake."

The two armored cars, and a third which had joined them covered the intersection. By the time Revell had pushed his way through to the bodies, the men of the column had stripped them of anything that could be remotely considered a souvenir.

Each of them hit by ten or more bullets, they lay grotesquely sprawled, half-naked, in mud largely composed of their own blood.

It was several minutes more before a group of camouflage-clad men came from the ambush point. There were seven in all, four of them were armed with general purpose machine guns.

They walked casually but confidently forward. Revell sensed they were more alert to their surroundings than their bearing suggested. Instinctively he picked out the officer among them, even though none wore any insignia.

"Your work?" He indicated the remains.

"Yes. Pip you at the post, did we? Saw you breaking in, figured we could get in first."

The officer patted the GPMG carried by the man next to him. "As you only had squirt guns, I thought you'd wait until they got in close. I'm Capt. Chester, 7th. Squadron Special Air Service. You'll be Major Revell; we were briefed you were in the area."

"Pity you weren't briefed that an infantry outfit was moving in as well."

Almost imperceptibly a shade of his self-assurance was shaved from the captain's manner. "Why's that."

"You had a firefight with them about an hour ago. Their fault as well, but they were the losers." Revell almost mentioned the shelter and the asphyxiated civilians, but decided against it.

"As far as we knew at that time, the city was a free-fire Zone. We'd only just landed."

"So, who's command are you under?" Revell had noted the radio backpack carried by one of the SAS men.

"Same as you will be, in about . . ." Chester looked up as a Black Hawk, with two gunships as escort, swept past overhead. ". . . about five minutes, I should say. My boss has been sent in to take over from the civil authority. Seems like the federal government believe the situation can be salvaged."

"I see. So such credit as there will be, is for them, is that it?" Revell thought of Police Chief Stadler, first hamstrung by military incompetence, and now deposed when the situation was within an ace of being remedied, or at least getting a lot closer to it.

"Not for me to say. Can't say I let politics bother me. I can tell you one thing though." Chester looked at the small police radio at the major's belt. "With more of our chaps due in soon, there's not going to be a lot more for you to do. Very nice of you to leave plenty of the Warpac warriors for us to deal with though. Thanks a lot."

"You going to take that shit, Major?" Dooley went to go after the captain as he walked away, but the officer's hand restrained him.

"We're not in the business of private feuds. He is right though. With an SAS staff running things, and sufficient units on the ground, all we're going to end up with is herding civilians."

"Great, let those supermen get the shitty end of the stick." Ripper looked back towards the furniture store. "I saw a king-size bed in there that is screaming to be tried out."

"Sergeant, let's take a stroll." At a little distance from the SAS soldiers, Revell used his radio to contact Stadler. "Might as well warn him what's coming. Chances are he doesn't know yet."

Stadler did know; a message had been relayed via the link with the airport. He was preparing to hand over, and that was all he told Revell before signing off.

"I don't blame him for being pissed off." Hyde sat on a traffic bollard, unfastened his helmet, and ran his hand back and forth over his head. It felt strange to be without it all of a sudden, after so long. "I don't mind living a bit longer, but I don't like being made redundant."

140

"Like it or not, we are."

Revell looked up as he heard the power traverse of an armored car turret start up. At the same moment, he noticed the sound of an approaching engine.

The column had begun to move out. Now the mixed force of airport police and security staff scattered in every direction, urgently seeking any cover they could find. Caught on the wrong side of the road, the SAS men ran from behind a trolley car to deploy their machine guns.

A sports car shot from a side street and swerved to avoid a group of men. It would also have missed the trees, but a ragged fusillade of shots sent it out of control, and glancing off one, it hit another head on.

Closest to the scene, Revell and Hyde dashed to the wreck. A middle-aged man was sprawled across the seat. His face was badly cut from his impact with the windshield, and both hands had been smashed by bullets.

"Looter?" Hyde helped pull him clear as flames began to lick from under the crumpled hood.

"Nein. No, I am not a looter."

Talking was an effort, and Revell judged by the quantity of blood issuing from the driver's mouth and nose that he'd suffered serious internal injuries.

"I was trying to get help. I thought you were more Russians."

"More?"

"Yes, ten of them, in the Theatiner Church. I escaped in the panic and confusion when the killing started."

CHAPTER TWENTY-SIX

It took Sgt. Hyde thirty-two seconds to round up the section, trying not to attract attention. The hardest part was extricating Andrea from a circle of admirers that included several of the SAS men. He was only just in time to prevent her committing some act of violence, going by her expression.

In the same length of time, Revell mounted the rear hull of the nearest armored car and put an argument forcefully to its commander.

The young lieutenant of the West German Territorials had been chafing at the bit, frustrated by the slow pace of the column, dictated by the excessive caution of his accompanying infantry. His English was no better than the major's German, but he understood what was wanted, and grinned at the prospect.

"Where you going, Major?" Capt. Chester ran to the Luchs, which Revell's section were boarding, finding handholds on the rear deck and hull sides. "This isn't the Second World War. You're not a tank-rider battalion. Where are you off to?"

"If you're needed, you'll get a call on the radio."

With that Revell had to hold on tight as the eight-wheeler surged forward, demolishing a steel post and driving over the top of it.

Fear was no stranger to Revell. He experienced it every time he went into action. This occasion it was particularly strong, almost overwhelming. If he could have thought of any other way into the church, even with acceptable civilian casualties, he would have employed that method rather than this.

The rear of the building was in shadow, as were the court-yard approaches to it. There would be enough of the late afternoon light for the Russians to see them. Hopefully not sufficient for them to be accurately identified.

When they had first arrived, there had been a couple of shots from inside, but there had been no more. The screaming and crying had continued though, and had jarred on the men's nerves.

Andrea alone had remained undisturbed, unmoved by the distress they could hear. She had got on with her preparations, seemingly able to blot out or ignore what she heard.

Not for any reason that he could understand, Revell neatly folded his camouflage jacket and webbing, propping his sub-machine gun carefully against the pile.

"Smelly sods, these Spetsnaz." Ripper sniffed the sleeve of the Russian battle dress.

"The particular sod who was wearing it spilt half his stomach and twenty-four hours of food and shit inside it. Your pants would stink after that." Carrington wrenched the unfamiliar webbing around until he had it settled more comfortably. "I'll be glad to get mine off as well though."

Revell made a last check. Three of them would be going in dressed as civilians, Andrea's presence helping that subterfuge. Carrington, Ripper, and Boris would be wearing the uniforms taken from the men they'd shot earlier in the day.

Dooley was having trouble getting into the clothes he'd selected. Having chosen what he thought was the right size, he now found that it wasn't. The jacket ended inches above his wrists, and the pants refused to meet round his waist.

"I'm going to be fucked if a fight starts and my slacks are round my knees." With a final tremendous effort, he managed to fasten his zip and secure the belt on the very last notch. "Shit, if I don't get zapped when my legs are tied together, I'm going to be strangled by these things. Are we ready, Major?"

"Pretty near." Revell handed Boris an AK47. He noticed the Russians hands were shaking almost uncontrollably. "Keep the safety on until the last moment. You're as likely to shoot yourself as a Stetsnaz."

"When you had me collected from the police station, Major, I thought it was only to carry out an interrogation. As you know, I am very good at — "

"Seeing as how you used to be in the Russian military police, you would be, wouldn't you. Have you got it straight, what to say?"

"Yes, Major. As little as possible. Keep behind and slightly to one side of you and the other, eh, civilians. Act a little drunk and mumble. Answer no direct questions. Get inside as fast as I can."

"Right." Feeling inside his loosely fitting windcheater, Revell checked the long-bladed knife in his belt. Against his right hip, he felt the comforting bulk of his pistol. "We're as ready as we're going to be."

From the church there came a babble of incoherent voices, and then a shot accompanied by a piercing scream. It ended with the sound of a second shot.

Behind them the rest of the section took up their places, covering all the rear exits from the church. At least they didn't have to worry about the front. Through Stadler, Revell had made sure that the WRACs across the road, still in place in the Residence, knew what was going down.

Anyone going out through the front was not going to get far. Of more immediate importance though, was how far Revell's party were going to get. A cautious reconnaissance had revealed that whatever the Russians in the church were up to, they weren't neglecting their security. How good it was they were about to discover for themselves.

"I never was any good in school drama productions. Best they ever cast me as was third spearman." Ripper liked the feel of the AK47. Better still, he liked the knowledge that being a Spetsnaz weapon, all its bullets would have a dumdum effect at target. If he hit what he aimed at, he wouldn't need to fire a second time.

144

"That's all you are right now, so you should be good at it." Carrington prodded Andrea with his automatic. "We're in sight of the bastard."

Boris felt the sweat pouring off him. He was sure the guard on the door would see, would know, that something was amiss. With the others he kept against the wall, hugging its shadow.

The challenge when it came was definitely slurred, but strong and carrying suspicion for all that.

Making his voice as weary and subdued as possible, Boris gave vent to a string of obscenity. It must have carried conviction. The guard waved them on. He was reaching out to Andrea, when Revell's saw-backed blade stabbed upwards under his chin and plunged in through his jaw, mouth, tongue, and palate.

The sudden weight against his arm told the major the shock of the blow had done its work. Twisting the knife as he withdrew it, he slid it in between two ribs to silently finish the job.

Hidden within the porch, the murder went unnoticed, and they stepped through into the heart of the church. The smell hit them at once. There was cordite and blood and slaughterhouse smells, but there was also an almost tangible scent of fear.

If anything, it was even darker inside, despite the mass of candles lit in every niche and on every ledge. There was one oasis of light, around the foot of the ornately carved wooden pulpit. It served to show the priest, arms outstretched, crucified with the hilts of knives sticking out of his palms.

At first there appeared to be fewer people there, then Revell realized they were all herded and crammed in at the alter end. A tall Russian was in the act of hauling a girl from the crowd when he saw who had entered. His questioning shout was aggressive and alerted other men near him.

Carrington gave Dooley a shove that sent the big man sprawling almost at the Russian's feet. It had the effect of defusing the situation for a moment. That was all that was needed.

145

CHAPTER TWENTY-SEVEN

The knife Dooley thrust with all his strength plunged in underneath the Russian's groin. He screeched in agony, jumping so violently that the blade pulled clear.

Jumping after him, Dooley had to deliver several more blows to finish him as he writhed and jerked. His further screams were drowned by the crash of fire from the escorts' Kalashnikovs and Revell's pistol.

Andrea found her own target. Her saw-backed blade slashed across the face and then the neck of a Russian who was grabbing for his rifle. Still he didn't go down, and her third lunge took an eye clean from its socket. The fourth blow she delivered to the base of his skull as he toppled.

Three had fallen to knives, four more went down in the hail of bullets that opened the attack. A fifth died as he went to take a shot from a choir stall, his head burst apart by the tumbling soft-nosed bullets.

"There are two more." A hastily aimed shot struck the stone by Revell's head, and sent a stinging hail of fragments into his neck.

He scanned the interior, but it was Carrington who spotted the sniper, high up at the back of a balcony. Three streams of steel converged on the screen behind which the Russian ducked for cover.

The ornate panelling splintered under the impact, but stayed in one piece. For a moment nothing happened, and then the screen toppled forward. Still standing behind it, the Russian swayed back and forth until a single shot struck him full in the chest and sent him crashing backwards out of sight.

Numbed into silence, there was no reaction from the civilians, not even when Dooley extracted the knives pinioning the priest and the poor man wailed as he slumped to the hard cold floor.

Revell had been searching the crowd for Sophia, afraid to look at the small heap of bodies behind the altar. At last he caught sight of her, hemmed in at the back.

"It's okay, we've got them. You're safe, you can move."

"No, no, I cannot. There are two more. One of them is behind me. He has a grenade."

Revell felt suddenly very cold. Casually, he took a half-step to the side. He could just make out the Russian. He was young. His face held a rigid expression that was part fear, part determination, but mostly it conveyed desperation.

"Boris, come here." Revell said it quietly, not turning to look for their deserter. "I want you here."

"Major, I heard what the young woman said. With a gun I might take a chance, but no one has ever outrun a grenade."

"Tell him it's all over. Tell him all his buddies are dead or captured. He's fighting a lost cause. Lost and futile." As he said it, Revell prayed there would not be the sound of gunfire from beyond the walls. If there were so much as a single shot, then the boy with the grenade, and little to lose, would know he was lying. Mercifully it stayed quiet.

"I have told him, Major. He says he does not care about the others. He has his duty."

How long would the Russian keep his grip on the bomb? Revell knew he must have a tight hold on it, so his fingers would cramp and his hand tire quickly. He saw the Russian lift his eyes to follow something higher up.

"No, don't." He didn't look, but Revell figured it would most likely be Andrea who was looking for a vantage point from which to shoot. "Boris, tell him he's not going to get out of this alive."

"He knows that, Major. He says he is prepared to die for

147

communism and Mother Russia."

"Ask him if he's prepared to die for a beer festival."

"He will think I am joking."

"He'll know I'm not. Tell him why today is a special day for Munich. Give it to him straight. I want him to know that his masters sent him in here to die, so that they could spoil a traditional West German booze-up."

The Russian listened. At first there was a contemptuous sneer on his face, as though he could hardly believe that such a pathetic tactic, so unbelievable a tale, would be tried. Gradually though, as Boris elaborated, doubt crept into his expression.

He jabbed and pushed at the frightened people about him, and questioned them in halting broken German. Many were too terrified to frame any sort of answer. Some by their eagerness made him suspicious again, but in one form or another he got similar answers from all who replied.

It grew darker in the church. By their contrast with the rapidly approaching night, the candles appeared the brighter. They moved and flickered in the drafts. Among the crowd a woman, or perhaps it was a man, began to sob. It was a low wracking sound that came from deep down. The priest was moaning quietly, and the two expressions of distress blended into an emotive background to the silent watch on the Russian.

At last, he stood up. The press of bodies about him parted as if by magic to let him out. He had gone only a few paces, when a shot rang out and echoed about the vaulted ceiling of the church.

The Russian crumpled, and as he did the grenade fell from his grasp. Those next three seconds were played out in horrific slow motion, filled with terror-stricken faces and frantic hopeless efforts to get away.

Shielded by the shallow step below the altar rail, Revell still felt the blast. Fragments passed so close he heard their superfast passage through the air. And he heard the ugly sound of

148

other jagged lumps of casing finding their mark among the press trying to escape.

The violence of the explosion passed quickly. The suffering it had created was going to last a long time. Thirty or more people had been grievously injured. They lay tangled together, many partially stripped of their clothes, some of their limbs.

Revell pulled bodies aside, sometimes finding they still lived and becoming more gentle with them. Many were almost unrecognizable, smothered as they were in blood and pieces of tissue and scraps of shredded clothing.

He found Sophia, half-covered by the altar cloth. She was already going cold. The back of her dress was a mass of red blotches.

"I saw him. He's gone up in the bell tower." Dooley helped Revell lift the girl's body and lay it on a strip of floor not speckled as yet with blood or too heavily littered with debris and scattered possessions.

"We've got him, Major." Carrington handed Revell an AK47 he'd picked up. "He can't escape. We've got him."

"No." Revell felt hate twist him up inside and turn him into someone he didn't recognize, into something that wasn't human.

"No, I've got him. He's mine."

CHAPTER TWENTY-EIGHT

The stairs climbed in a series of short steep flights. Before starting up, Revell listened intently. Not all the rage inside him could blot out his experience of this type of fighting, and he brought it all into play.

As the staircase turned to the right, he transferred his pistol to his left hand. He was not such a good shot that way, but the change would enable his weapon to cover a greater arc as he climbed. The inevitably short range of any engagement would also help to compensate.

There was no sound from above, and he started up, one step at a time. He transferred his weight carefully from one foot to the other, making sure at all times that he was perfectly balanced.

Still he had no indication of how close the Russian might be, and then as he came within a few steps of the third landing, he heard a repetitive bumping. He knew what it was before he saw the fragmentation grenade. It rolled to a stop against an angle of the wall, and he caught the briefest glimpse of the cylindrical green bomb before ducking as low as he could.

A fraction of a delay, and then the device detonated. Dust poured from every crevice, and pieces of casing zipped from the walls and stairs.

Before the thunder of the echo had died, Revell had snatched a concussion grenade from his belt, extracted the pin, counted off a brief delay, and then lobbed it upward as hard as he could.

It was a dangerous tactic, but all the more likely to succeed because it would be unexpected. With a crash the grenade burst, and at the instant it did, Revell was moving upwards as fast as he could in the severely reduced visibility.

As he neared the top, he snapped off single shots into the dust-enhanced gloom ahead. There were no answering reports.

Eyes streaming and lungs gasping for air, Revell reached the first of the shuttered windows. Fighting down his labored gasping breath, he peered into the murk. Crouching down, he fired across the interior of the tower, and heard his own bullet ricochet madly back past his ear.

The fog was clearing fast, and he felt a strong gust of air on his face. An eddy in the rapidly dispersing dust cloud revealed a shutter gaping open, immediately opposite him.

From outside came the sound of a body landing, and hands scrabbling for grip on a pitched roof. When he reached the opening, he could just make out a dark form moving rapidly across the roof, working up towards the ridge at a tangent.

Revell fired the rest of the magazine as fast as he could, feeling the Browning's heavy recoil as he sent each 9mm round at the Russian.

One of the bullets must have found its mark. The figure reared up, and a rifle clattered away down the roof and over the edge to the long drop into the street.

The Russian didn't follow the weapon, instead he managed to get a hand to the ridge and began to haul himself up.

Revell dropped from the window onto the roof. The

drop was longer than he expected, and he lost his balance and was winded as he fell sideways against the brickwork of the tower. Instinctively his hand went to the butt of his knife. It was still there. Taking it out of its sheath, he settled it firmly in the palm of his hand before starting up the slope.

Above him the wounded Russian had managed to get astride the ridge and was using both hands to pull his injured leg over.

"I've got you!" Revell hurled himself the last few yards and was about to lunge at his target when the muzzle flash of a pistol dazzled him.

His night vision gone, Revell only heard, not saw, the second shot fired. It too missed at point-blank range, but he felt the heavy rour _ cut along the side of his Kevlar helmet, almost ripping it away. Wildly he lashed out in a long slashing cut with the blade, and felt it connect.

It was only out of the corners of his vision that Revell could see. To look straight ahead was to experience again the searing light of the muzzle flash. Risking everything, he let go with his left hand of the projection he'd been clutching and grabbed blindly for his opponent.

His fingers brushed and then held tight a wad of material. The butt of a pistol came down hard, first on his helmet and then on his shoulder. Twice the blow was repeated, and he felt his arm going numb. In a last desperate attempt, he once more slashed upwards with the knife.

Again it connected, this time deeply penetrating flesh and muscle that he felt constrict and grip the blade. Wrenching it hard, at the same moment he felt another smashing blow.

Before any more could be landed and his collarbone broken, Revell threw all his weight against the knife. He

152

could feel it grating along bone as it stripped cartiledge away and severed arteries.

There was a metallic bump, and the pistol slid off the roof. Strong hands fastened on Revell's neck, and his head was forced back as they tightened their grip. Still he held the knife, driving it ever deeper into tissue.

The major's face was only inches from the Russian's, he could smell whiskey on his breath, but only see him in outline against the lighter western sky. With all his effort concentrated on it, the knife had now slit the Russian's leg open from mid-thigh to knee, but he showed no sign of weakening. If anything, the stranglehold was becoming tighter.

Only the corner of the flakjacket's collar caught beneath the throttling fingers prevented them cutting off his air completely. Even so, he could feel his head starting to swim, his senses to reel, and he knew he couldn't hold on much longer.

With all the effort he could muster, he pushed up hard with his feet. His left hand let go the hold on the Russian's clothing, and his fingers jabbed for the man's face. One found his eye, and there was a scream.

Thrashing about, the Russian overbalanced and as he toppled, he took Revell with him. They slid down the roof, locked together.

At the edge, Revell managed to grab hold of a stone statue. For an instant his adversary's webbing caught on the same projection, then slid free, and he was gone. As he consolidated his hold, Revell heard the ugly sound of a heavy landing far below.

Resting awhile before making the attempt, Revell hauled himself into the valley between the roof and the tower. He would not have been able to make the next move—raising himself at the full stretch of his arms into

153

the window—if others had not gripped him and assisted.

"That the last of them, Major?" Dooley handed over his water bottle.

As Revell swigged deeply, feeling the tepid water sluice the dust from his lips and throat, he heard a furious outbreak of firing from the other side of the city center.

"That was the last of that bunch. But it doesn't sound like the body count is complete yet."

CHAPTER TWENTY-NINE

The number of civilians on the street was increasing. More and more were leaving the shelters in search of food or medical help. Others were trying to get back to their apartments or hotel rooms for a wash and a change of clothing, or to check that their property was not the booty of looters.

Armed civilian gangs were on the streets also. Most had only improvised weapons, but some had obtained guns or even crossbows from sporting goods stores.

The majority were on foot, but people who could get to their cars — and thieves who could get one started — were trying to leave the city.

Attempts were being made to get food and drink to those still in the shelters. Much of it was being "requisitioned" from food stores and restaurants. Sometimes the owners would appear and engage in vitriolic slanging matches with police organizing the depredations.

There were all the ingredients for a disaster, and on a local scale at least, it was beginning to happen. On Ludwigstrasse police trying unsuccessfully to control a mob fired shots in the air. A nearby Panzer grenadier section thought they were coming under fire and opened up. It took twenty minutes for the mistake to be recognized. By then there were thirty dead and twice as many wounded.

"The city is coming apart at the seams." Mayor Gebert surveyed the bodies being dragged to the side of the road.

The police car he had been using to visit parts of the city cleared of the Spetsnaz forces sat quietly steaming on its flat front tires in a barber shop doorway. The stump of a crossbow bolt still projected from a sidewall.

Revell and his men had arrived too late to tackle the band of looters. They could only put a cordon about the area, until an ambulance arrived for the driver. Not that there was much chance of the criminals returning. The jewelry store they had been disturbed in the act of cleaning out had nothing but display pads remaining on show.

The steel grill formerly protecting the windows had been wrenched aside and the alarm clamored shrilly, until Burke put several rounds into it. Even then it continued to produce a subdued tinny rattle.

"I thought we were getting on top of the situation?"

"We are, Major, but the cost is escalating too far, too fast."

There was still the sound of shooting coming from other quarters, but allowing for the fact that some of it would be between police and looters, the number of Spetsnaz engaged seemed smaller.

Listening intently, Revell decided that the nearest gun battle was several blocks away. "Do we know how many of them dropped into the city?"

"You don't seriously think the military are keeping me informed, do you?" Gebert was contemptuous. "One of my . . . one of Stadler's SWAT teams took a prisoner. He was removed by a GSG9 antiterrorist squad. I don't know what technique they used, but after they interrogated him, they declared that a hundred Spetsnaz had made the drop."

Revell snorted his disbelief.

"I agree. I knocked the arrogance out of them by telling them that a police sweep of the park had revealed one-hundred-and-ninety-six canopies. The Reds hadn't bothered to try hiding them. Too keen to get on, I suppose."

"So, allowing for a handful to have gone astray, my first guess of about two hundred won't be far from the mark." Revell felt pleased with himself.

"Yes, I mentioned your estimate. I am afraid that proving the elite units wrong may not have added to your popularity with them. Hence . . ." Gebert swept his hand in a gesture that took in the deserted street and the disabled police vehicle.

"Do you know who, besides the SAS, is in on it now?"

Gebert looked to where his driver was vainly trying to staunch the flow of blood from his bullet-pierced earlobe. "Not everyone. SAS are certainly in command, but they're too thin on the ground to hog the whole show to themselves, so they've grudgingly allowed two squads of GSG9, Stadler's SWAT teams, and a platoon of Bundeswehr Airborne Infantry to join in."

"Generous of them. Are they getting results?" Revell saw the tracer of a cannon shell smack into the top storey of a tower block a kilometer off.

"That's another reason you're not popular. They're keeping a score board. Going solely on actual body count, your Special Combat Company is in the lead. The police would actually be at the top, but each of their kills is being chalked up as a separate engagement."

"How accurate is the tally then?" Revell had a lot of experience of field commanders and higher ups, falsifying body counts. He'd known them not just be doubled, but increased as much as tenfold.

"That I have to give them." Gebert moved on to the sidewalk as an army ambulance pulled up, accompanied by a pickup crammed with armed police. "They are only allowing verified kills. When I left, they were waiting for the fire brigade to get into a burning school before adding what they believe to be three more to the sheet."

The urge to ask the total had to be fought down by

157

Revell. Gebert was shrewd enough to know the question he wanted to pose.

"One-hundred-and-fifty-seven when I left twenty minutes ago. The cost is mounting enormously though. I do not mean that in a monetary sense." Watching the driver being assisted to the rear of the Land Rover ambulance, Gebert dismissed he smashed front of the jewelers.

"As yet we do not have a figure for civilian casualties. It is likely though that it will rise into the hundreds, I think."

Revell considered telling him about the shelter with its suffocated inmates, but decided against it. Soon enough he would learn the death toll was well into the thousands.

The ambulance departed with its overburdened escort vehicle. As it left a police crew bus arrived with a motorcycle escort.

"I suppose you'll be kicking your heels for a while." Gebert went to board the vehicle. "Until they find some routine task for you."

"I expect so." Revell knew that to be more than likely. "In the minds of a lot of the military—even outfits like SAS and Delta Force—we're considered to be no better than a private army."

"Then if I ever need one, I'll know where to come, will I not."

Revell watched Gebert depart on the next stage of his inspection tour. He didn't envy the mayor. When all this was over, there were going to be a lot of people wise after the event. Mostly it would be those who were out of town, or who, now skulking in the recesses of a deep shelter, would appoint themselves as critical analysts of what had happened.

Heads would roll, both among the military and political circles, where blame could thought to be attached. Only the administrators would escape the condemnation that would follow the inquest likely to be conducted by the media. Snug in their town hall offices, exempt from military service, comfortable with the expectation of their indexed pensions, they would ride out the storm of criticism.

Checking in by radio, Revell was told only to stand by. For what, or when any task could be expected, he wasn't informed.

"Sgt. Hyde." Well if they were going to be kept hanging about, there was no reason why they couldn't do it with a degree of comfort. "Find us a decent hotel. There's no point in us bumbling about when we're not wanted. We'll only get our heads shot off. Let's put our feet up for a while."

"This lot gets too comfortable, Major, they'll probably fall asleep. It'll be a hell of job waking them."

"That's a chance I'll take. Make it somewhere close at hand. Don't consult Ackerman though. My stomach is still rebelling over that food at the restaurant he found."

Sitting on the hood of the abandoned police car, Revell took off his helmet and fingered the long crease in the layered material. The high velocity round had cut a neat furrow in it.

It wasn't the first time one had come that close. With luck, though it might be the last in Munich.

CHAPTER THIRTY

From the rooftop restaurant, Revell had a panoramic view of the city. Most of it was blacked out still, but here and there an imperfectly curtained window let slip a sliver of light.

And there were the fires. He counted at least eight. While most showed as no more than a glow over the rooftops, there was a large conflagration in the general direction of the fairground. If indeed it was some or all of the rides and sideshows that were going up, the mass of painted and varnished wood would make for a spectacular blaze.

Down in the streets there was more traffic than he might have expected. Fire engines, ambulances, and police cars made up a large part of it. There were military vehicles also. Mostly it was armored cars, but he saw a couple of wheeled APC's and a single self-propelled gun.

That unwieldy monster was making slow progress, and was led and flanked by a large number of military police Hummers and motorcycles. Revell watched it until it was out of sight.

"If they try using that, the repair bill is going to be higher." Andrea straddled a chair and began to pull the well-crisped skin off of a drumstick.

"The threat of its employment should be sufficient. I imagine it'll be used to winkle out the last stubborn few."

They were alone. None of the others had bothered to take the lift to the top floor. In all the hotel they had encountered only two staff — a pair of hopelessly inebriated waiters — in the cocktail bar. With no doors locked the rest of the men

160

had found all that they needed on the ground floor.

Revell remembered another time, when he had stood looking out over another city. That had been Hamburg, from the top of the television tower. Then his companion had been another beautiful woman, Inga.*

Hamburg had been destroyed when the Zone had rolled forward to surround and engulf it. Inga had died with the city. He wondered if Andrea ever thought of Hamburg, as he so often did. It was she who had discovered that Inga was a Russian agent . . . and killed her.

"What are you thinking?"

He'd never expected her to ask him that. His instinctive reaction was to think of something, anything, rather than what had been in his mind. Then he rejected that.

"I was thinking of Hamburg . . ."

"And the girl Inga?"

"Yes, I was. We stood and looked out at the city, just like this."

"You know I killed her."

Andrea's tone was flat, emotionless. He wondered if she was trying to goad some reaction from him. If so, she would fail. The event was long in the past, the thought of it did not touch him anymore.

"Why do you think I killed her?"

Again a question he could not have anticipated. She was acting very differently tonight. Had she been drinking, before joining him up here? There was no way he could tell, unless he detected it on her breath. In the past though, alcohol had made her even more withdrawn than her usual taciturn self.

"You found out that she was an agent. I know that. With your hatred of all things communist, did you need any other reason?"

Down in the street, a Marder tracked APC trundled past. Its commander was risking using dipped headlights. That

*ZONE 5: OVERKILL.

could be a fatal mistake Revell thought, with enemy snipers in action. But then the Marder had decent armored protection, at least against small-arms fire. The commander would have to stay closed down though. Even with all the sophisticated night vision devices he had available, that still brought other penalties . . . Revell realized he was deliberately letting his mind be sidetracked, avoiding the conversation, trying not to hear her words.

"I enjoyed killing her, but not just because of what she was. She told me all of the things you had done together. I made her. Have I told you that before ? I think the drinking I have done has affected my memory, but I am not drunk now."

Revell turned to her, and found she was looking at him. "Was Sophia right about you? Or are you just a frustrated cock-teaser?"

"Perhaps I am a lesbian. When I was quite young, I had a special friend. She used to stay at my house at weekends. We would share a bed. I liked her touching me, and I did the same for her."

"Why all the soul-baring?" Her conversation was so unlike any he'd ever had with her, he felt out of his depth.

"That I cannot tell you, because I do not know. I just felt I had to talk. As I know how you feel about me, I thought you would at least listen, without reacting to the sexual arousal you might experience at such a conversation."

"I am human. Why do you think I would have more control than any other man?"

"Oh, I am not talking about control." Andrea undid her belt. "Self-discipline I would expect you to have." She unfastened her jacket. "You will not grab me because I am a dream you have. Touch me, yes. Watch me masturbate, yes. But to go all the way?"

Revell didn't take his eyes off her as she removed her jacket and threw it carelessly across a smart table setting.

"If you do that, what other dream do you have to replace

162

it? You are a soldier, your battles are fought in the Zone, most of the time." Andrea glanced out at the city. "For you there is no dream of comfortable retirement. You will not live to pensionable age, and you know it. So you made me your dream, your something to look forward to."

"You're presuming a hell of a lot." It was like she was reading his mind, but even that he couldn't admit. Like so much else he repressed it, pushed it aside. "So if this is what you believe, why bring it up? Why chose this time and place?"

"Because I feel there will not be another. Out there they are still fighting. I know you do not think so, but somehow I know this city has not finished with us yet."

"A premonition, is that what you're saying?"

"Give it what label you like. Call it the fabled woman's intuition if you prefer. I only tell you what I feel inside."

"If you were right, is there anything I could do to prevent something happening?" Revell searched for a word. "Preordained, isn't that what it's called?"

Andrea looked hard at the major, trying to determine if he was having fun at her expense. Certainly he was smiling, but not in derision. It was a sad smile, like he was sorry for both of them.

"I've never shattered a dream before, especially not one of my own," Revell looked towards the lifts, "and we might be discovered, I mean disturbed . . ."

"You will not like it as much if we had more time and comfort." Andrea sank down on her knees, then rolled sideways to lay full length on her back. Her hands began to edge her clothing lower.

"Please, don't tell me what I will and won't like. Don't try to do my thinking for me." As her legs parted, Revell knelt beside her. He had seen her body before, watched her working it with her fingers to a climax.

While inside he screamed at himself to go faster, his shell moved slowly. She was right about him not liking the dis-

163

comfort. Improvised lovemaking had never been to his taste. It least though, by not hurling himself straight on top of her, he could salvage some tiny measure of satisfaction of more than just carnal needs.

Andrea knew what he was doing, sensed his need to get more from this, their first intercourse, than the quick fulfillment of a physical need. She did not try to hurry him when he gently brushed his lips against hers, though she realized how little time they had. His actions called for no response on her part, not even when he lightly ran his fingertips across her stomach, between her legs, and then on to her thigh. Laying still she waited, feeling his erection warm against her leg.

Surely she should have felt more than this. Bracing herself to take his weight as he moved on top of her, she was surprised at how little discomfort there was; the effort he made to support himself.

"This is the first time . . . with a man." The words came without her planning them. They surprised her, and she waited for his reaction.

At the moment the tip of his penis entered her body, he checked for an instant. Then he was pushing into her. His mind was in turmoil. He had speculated, for so long, to himself. Not that he could ever have hoped . . . *if* she was telling the truth.

Beyond the windows a whole city was struggling to survive. On the floor in the deserted restaurant, two people were managing to forget it existed.

CHAPTER THIRTY-ONE

"Can you trust him?"

The SAS Colonel stalked from behind his desk and glared at Boris, though it was Revell he spoke to.

"So far I've had no reason to think otherwise."

"Shit, shit, fucking shit." Col. Granger looked at the document that Boris had just translated. "At least it confirms what we've obtained from interrogations. And it almost matches the number of chutes that have been retrieved."

"It matches exactly." Revell noticed that the Russian was edging towards the door. "The Police have spotted two canopies on the roof of the Olympic Stadium. Bodies are still attached." He saw Boris finally manage to sidle from the room.

The Colonel didn't bother to add the figures again. The body count stood at one hundred and ninety exactly. All the available evidence indicated that a total of two hundred and two Spetsnaz troops had made the drop.

"What about those snipers you engaged ? You claimed no kills. Where was it ? Oh yes, a side street hotel and the bank on Marienplatz. So how about it, think you're being pessimistic?"

"I'd like to think I'm being realistic."

"Could the bodies have been destroyed by the fire or explosion?"

"I couldn't say, Colonel. I stick by what I know for sure. We left the hotel starting to burn nicely. On Marienplatz we scored a direct hit. We got no more fire from either location, but that doesn't say that the Reds had hung about waiting for us to hit them."

"In both cases I'm waiting for police and fire brigade reports. Do you think you got two sections with those hits?" Granger rubbed his hands hopefully.

"I'd think it highly unlikely. We weren't utilizing that sort of firepower."

A motorcycle messenger entered and handed the colonel a paper. He unfolded it, and had to turn it hand over hand to get it the right way up.

"Shit, fucking shit. You missed them."

Revell wasn't about to labor the point again. If the colonel chose to persist in deluding himself by thinking that Revell and his unit had put in false claims, then let him. He truly didn't care any more. He was too tired and had too many other things on his mind.

"We're still missing twelve of the bastards."

"Maybe they've deserted. Taken vehicles and skipped, right out of the city, perhaps. After all, we ran into a few who were trying just that."

"Because you've seen a lot of men do that in the Zone, it doesn't mean every unit is likely to disintegrate if it gets half a chance."

"I wasn't suggesting that, Colonel." Revell could kick himself for suggesting anything. "But I do think we're helping the Russians by building up this superman image of their Spetsnaz troops."

"You're an authority, you've fought them before?"

"No, all I'm saying is that I don't believe the Russians have managed to build up and maintain elite troops trained to the standards that these are rumored to have achieved." Revell sought an example, and found an obvious one. "How about your outfit? Even with years of preparation, do you think you could find and train upwards of thirty thousand men to your standards?"

Col. Granger had flushed an angry red when the major had started speaking; gradually he managed to bring his temper under control. "So what are they then, boy scouts . . . ?

"Simply well-trained troops who've had a good PR campaign organized for them in the West. Among them will be the good, the bad, and the deserters."

"Fortunately I don't subscribe to your theory, Major. I believe they will be holed up somewhere in the city center, waiting for things to get back to normal, before popping up again."

"You could be falling into a trap, Colonel, one of your own making. You work on that supposition, and you'll be tying up troops and snarling up the city for a long time to come."

Revell could see the colonel was not about to be convinced, but felt he had to give it one more try.

"They've had plenty of time to make a run. They could have stolen transport, or hidden and waited to mingle with the first of the crowds coming from the shelters. Easy enough for them to obtain civy gear."

"That's enough, Major. I'll take care of matters my way. Don't you have some transport waiting?"

For a moment, Revell stood his ground, then tiredness and apathy swept over him. What the hell, it wasn't his fight any longer. Maybe he should make one more try. No, the hell he would.

Abruptly, Revell left the room. In the outer office he collected Boris. He was not alone. There were a number of the colonel's troops there, all tough-looking heavily armed men. Their proximity was clearly causing Boris considerable distress. His manner was nervous and agitated.

"Major." Boris hissed out the corner of his mouth as they went out. "In the last few hours, you have made me go up against drunken Spetsnaz, and sit in a room with ten SAS men. My bowels will not take what you are putting them through."

"You'll be okay. We're finished with Munich. Transport is laid on. We leave as soon as we're boarded."

"Then my only regret is that it was not thirty-six hours sooner."

Going out through the front door, Boris walked straight

into an SAS machine gunner draped with belts of ammunition. He jumped, apologized in Russian, and then went deadly pale as he realized what he'd done.

By the time Revell was outside, Boris was already two blocks away.

Munich was returning to normal at an almost frenetic pace. Battalions of city employees were sweeping the streets, and squadrons of tow trucks removing burned-out, smashed, and abandoned cars. Damaged storefronts were being boarded over with sheets of pastel-colored ply, giving the appearance of undergoing refit, rather than being hidden from the gawp of tourists.

True, there were more police on the street than was usual, but not exceptionally so, a few APCs parked in side streets, but that wasn't such an unusual sight. Only the frequent roadblocks, where the identification of every man was double-checked, were out of the ordinary.

A few side streets were cordoned off, and the taint of smoke hung over the city, but the smell permeating the pedestrian malls was more likely to come from hot dog stalls and hamburger stands than buildings being damped down.

The main railroad station was still closed, after the destruction of its signal cabin by an overenthusiastic application of force by an SAS team. It was by truck that the Special Combat Company was to be moved.

There was no one to see them leave, bar the passing pedestrians, and they took no notice of so common a sight. The last men were climbing aboard, when a military police station wagon pulled up in front of the lead vehicle. Two police cars boxed in the little convoy at the back.

"Bloody hell." From the back of the tail-end Bedford, Scully watched the police approach their officer. "This doesn't look like a social visit."

"Perhaps they're going to bill us for any damage we've

168

done." Burke's tone was caustic.

"Sure as fuck they haven't brought a vote of thanks from the city fathers."

Dooley watched the conversation between the major and the officers. It was short, almost curt. During it Revell's expression hardened. At its conclusion, he laid his submachine gun on the ground and emptied a pocket of shells. An MP pointed to his holster, and when Revell shook his head, a police officer stepped forward and reached for the pistol.

"They're arresting the major!"

The shout Dooley gave as he jumped out was heard along the line of trucks. Suddenly every member of the company was leaping down and making for the rear of the convoy.

Seeing the numbers advancing on them, the police fell back their to their cars. For a while, the four MPs stood their ground, until they were pushed and jostled against a store window that bowed ominously under the pressure. One of them tried to draw his side arm, but had it wrenched from his hand, unloaded, and then thrust back at him hard.

Two of them pulled their clubs, but those too they were relieved of, but those weren't returned, disappearing instead into the encircling crowd.

Civilians, sensing trouble, scurried away. A police officer attempting to use his car radio had the handset pulled from his grasp and ripped out, complete with its coiled lead.

"Hold it, hold it." Revell had to bellow at the top of his voice to make himself heard above the threats being hurled at police and MPs. "Back off, all of you."

CHAPTER THIRTY-TWO

The pile of firearms on the sidewalk grew as the men handed in the weapons they had obtained in the city. Revell stood to one side, watching the process.

In turn each man would step forward, unload, show the breach of his weapon was empty, and add it to the stack. The first few had thrown the rifles and submachine guns down hard, obviously hoping to damage them. When the lieutenant in charge of the military police detachment protested, Revell had to order more care taken.

It was an impressive collection, and the assortment of grenades and ammunition beside it was no less daunting.

"That's everything. We can go now?" Revell got no reply. The police were totally absorbed in worried contemplation of the heap of ordnance they'd suddenly inherited. "Oh, one last item."

The police jumped back in alarm as a tattered flak jacket landed among, and scattered, bullets and bombs.

It was as they started to drive north out of the city, that Revell began to realize just what effect the Russian assault had created. The road was packed with vehicles of every description. Anything that would drive, and for which fuel could be found, was taking part in a huge exodus.

Every car, truck, and bus was piled high with luggage, and packed tight with passengers. Bumper to bumper the traffic crawled away from Munich.

At the cost of two hundred troops, the Soviets had crippled a vital war production center. Many of those leaving had not been anywhere near the fighting that had taken place. The majority had at most only seen the smoke or heard a faint echo of the gunfire.

This fleeing mass was on the move because its nerve had snapped. Living on the edge of the Zone for so long had taken its toll. The carefully calculated attack, its surgically precise objective had succeeded and been achieved.

Munich wasn't going to disintegrate, not today, perhaps not next month, but inevitably it would. The Oktoberfest would go on, starting a couple of days late. Attendence would be down, but probably not noticeably so, considering what had happened.

In days the scars of battle would be gone, the blaring headlines forgotten by all but those who lost family or friends, or whose business had suffered.

What was beyond recovery was the production at the armorments factories. Many immigrant workers would shift to other production centers, but a significant proportion would be lost, returning home.

And those who stayed, those without the courage to uproot themselves, or those too stubborn to do so, they would be looking over their shoulder all the time they worked. They would worry about their families, about their future.

From this time onwards, the Warpac bombers would only have to stray a few meters outside of the Zone to trigger an air raid warning. The inevitable reaction in Munich would shut down the city for hours or even days.

The convoy moved slowly north. In an hour they had covered barely six kilometers. They were still within the city's suburbs.

Riding in the cab of the leading truck, Revell gradually became more and more aware of the driver's preoccupation with the temperature gauge. He wasn't surprised when they pulled off the road and on to the forecourt of a service station.

While their truck joined the queue for the water hose, Revell waved the rest of the column to park on the verge. Many of the

171

men took advantage of the stop to stretch their legs. Several also took the opportunity to go behind a paling fence and relieve themselves.

A few private cars were also pulling in to fill up at the pumps. Revell watched them idly while he waited. It was a self-service gas station, and after getting out, each driver would go through much the same ritual.

After unlocking their filler caps, they would look at the pumps. Inevitably noticing that the previous sale was still registered, they would look towards the pay booth. A short impatient wait would be followed by a fruitless visit to the cash desk, and then a return to the car.

Vehicles holding several passengers always became the scene of an urgent discussion. The culmination of that was usually the quick topping-up of the tank, followed by a hurried departure. Not many made a second visit to the booth to push through the correct money and the necessary accompanying fuel ration coupons.

Hyde had also been watching what was going on. He joined the major. "You wouldn't think this place would be deserted, at a time like this, would you? I'd have expected them to be charging well over the odds, grabbing all the profit they can."

Revell looked up at the company logo. "It belongs to one of the big groups. The staff don't give a damn. They're probably a few kilometers ahead of us in traffic."

"I suppose so, but it just doesn't feel right somehow." Hyde looked towards the booth. I'll just take a look around."

In the car wash, Hyde discovered two bodies. They were those of a woman in her early twenties and a little girl. Dragged inside, they had been dumped carelessly on the concrete floor. When he called his officer over, he pointed out the nature of their injuries.

"The woman has been shot in the back from close range. Didn't waste bullets on the kid. Looks like she was clubbed. Smashed in her skull. This would be the work of looters, I suppose."

172

"I don't think so." Revell felt the bodies. They still retained some body heat. "I peeped in the booth. The cash register is still packed with notes, and there's a mass of coupons. Single-shot execution isn't looters' style either."

Hyde knew what the major was thinking. "No, that's Spetsnaz style, when they haven't got time to indulge in a spot of rape or torture."

"My very thoughts. This couldn't have happened more than thirty minutes ago. The bodies are still warm."

"She must have kicked up a fuss when they stopped for gas." Hyde looked again at the child. Her face and blonde hair were smothered in blood that had oozed from a gash at the center of a massive depressed fracture. "They must have taken the woman out quick, and then bashed the kiddie when she saw what was happening."

It was difficult for Revell to be certain, but he had the impression that the traffic was flowing even slower than it had been when they pulled off. "If they grabbed their transport in Munich, then they don't have cross-country capability. That means they're forced to stick to the roads, and we can catch them."

"There are thousands of vehicles. If they've changed into civies, how the hell are we going to find them?"

"We'll flush them out. How many weapons did we manage to keep back altogether?" Revell recalled the MP5 he had wedged under the passenger seat on the Beford.

"Eight submachine guns, sixteen full magazines. And Andrea kept a hold of four phosphorus and two fragmentation grenades."

"It'll have to be sufficient. Get our best section out on the road. We're going hunting."

CHAPTER THIRTY-THREE

With a typical German respect for the rules, the traffic had confined itself to the three north-bound lanes. Hardly any drivers took advantage of the occasional gaps in the central crash barriers to get on to the deserted south-bound carriageways.

One that had already regretted the decision. A Citroen, displaying French licence plates, had collided head on with a Mercedes belonging to the autobahn police.

As Revell and his group advanced on foot between the rows of cars, they made no attempt at concealment, even deliberately making great show of the weapons they carried. They shouted back and forth between themselves, and had early proof that the tactic could be effective.

Twice within the first kilometer, their noisy progress flushed looters from cars up ahead. The first time it was three girls. They abandoned a near new Audi and raced up an embankment. As they went, they dropped a trail of boxes of perfume, jewelry and leather jackets.

When Dooley passed their vehicle, he reached in, grabbed an atomizer, and sprayed himself generously with Chanel. "Want not, waste not."

A little further on, he handed the remainder of the spray to a young girl gaping from the open window of a Saab. He got a scowl from her father who sat behind the wheel. As soon as he was past, he heard the bottle break on the road, and the window being wound closed.

The second group of looters they unwittingly stumbled across was a different proposition. When the nearest of the section was still a hundred meters off, they suddenly swung their big Volvo hard into the car beside them, bulldozed past it, and tried to escape.

They got only as far as a wire mesh fence at the top of the steep-sided cutting they were in. Wheels spinning on the soft turf, the heavy car could make no impression on the obstruction, and began to dig itself into the ground. It sent up fans of grass and soil as the tires failed to find a grip.

Throwing open the doors, five male occupants jumped out. The last to do so carried a shotgun. He blasted with both barrels towards the road, then fumbled to reload.

The response to the brief burst fired over their heads by Revell was to throw their hands in the air. Then, uncomprehendingly, they watched as the soldiers stalked past and ignored them.

Once they realized that they were not being arrested, the men suddenly threw themselves into ill-organized frantic activity. While one of their number attacked the fence with wire cutters, another hurled himself back inside, and the rest put their shoulders to the rear of the car.

Part of the section's rearguard, Andrea watched the looters' strenuous efforts. "Such a lot of work, and for what?"

"Who knows." Ripper was tempted to take a potshot, but resisted the urge. "But whatever it is, by the time they've sold it for a tenth of what it's worth, and split the proceeds between five of them, it's only going to be worth beer money."

Andrea saw one of the men go to pick up the shotgun. She didn't wait to see if he intended to use it. Her three-round burst broke his back and he crumpled, screaming, onto the trampled grass.

The others piled into the Volvo as it began to nudge through the fence. Andrea was about to fire again, but remembered their shortage of ammunition. She had to watch the car disappear from sight.

Ripper knocked on the driver's window of the vehicle that

had been rammed. A white-faced woman sat still gripping the wheel. Three young children were crying and fighting in the rear.

"Your car's wrecked, lady. If you go back down the road a ways, you'll find an Audi no one is using."

Walking on, neither of them saw the crippled looter finally get his fingers to the trigger of the shotgun. Tormented by the excruciating pain of his wounds, he jabbed the twin barrels into his mouth, and fired.

It was a gamble, but Revell was putting everything on the Russians continuing to try and blend in with the fleeing population of Munich.

He knew that at any time the Reds could swing out of the stream of traffic and make faster progress by using the unobstructed south-bound lanes. He had to count on their not doing that. His hope was that they would realize their best chance of getting clear of the area lay in staying with the herd.

There would be police checkpoints somewhere up ahead. With such a heavy flow of traffic, there was no way every vehicle and its occupants could be scrutinized. Once over that hurdle, the Spetsnaz could head off in any direction.

Each time the section approached a large truck or bus, Revell felt his stomach start to churn. It was a familiar sensation—fear. If the Russians were cornered, they would very likely fight to the last man.

A gun battle among the lines of cars—most laden with whole families—would be horrific. The main hope of avoiding that lay in the section's ostentatious advance spurring the enemy to make a break for it.

They moved on steadily. Here the autobahn ran through the center of derelict land. It must once have been a vast switching yard. There was little sign of it remaining. Broad swathes of concrete and ballast, broken only by intruding

176

clumps of weeds, alternated with patches of stunted shrubs.

On the far side stood a vast clutter of stainless steel towers, a chemical plant. Flanking it, and stretching away out of sight, were the globes and tanks of a storage farm.

Above a slim stack, a flare burned brightly against the overcast sky. Plumes of steam rose from long runs of piping. Warning lights marked the top of the taller structures.

A half kilometer ahead, Revell saw a big road junction. On a flyover that crossed the interchange, the flashing lights of police vehicles were seen. If the Spetsnaz had already managed to bluff their way through the roadblock, then the whole of West Germany lay open to them. But if they had not reached it yet, then within the next ten minutes the section would come up on them.

Scanning the autobahn ahead, Revell noticed a single-deck bus. It was a large six-wheeler, of the type designed for long distance travel. Most of its curtains were closed. Though one or two were not, it was impossible to see in through the tinted glass.

"If they're anywhere, that's where they'll be."

Revell was happy to hear his thoughts echoed by his sergeant. He eased off the safety catch on his MP5. With all the mental power he could summon, he was willing the Russians to make a run for it. Hemmed in as it was, there was no chance of the bus crashing clear.

At the front end of the long vehicle, an automatic door folded back and steps came down. Revell could guess what was coming.

There was a lot of shouting and cries of fright and pain as the civilian passengers were forced out. With the Russian soldiers mingled among them, they threaded their way between the cars and trucks. Threats and brutality were employed to move the group off the autobahn.

"You keep back."

Revell didn't see who it was who shouted. He heard a shot

177

and saw an elderly man crumple. Blood spurted from a gaping head wound. Again a heavily accented voice came from among the hostages.

"You keep back, or we make a lot more like that."

CHAPTER THIRTY-FOUR

Rifle butts and boots were used to club and kick the captive civilians to silence. Among them a woman sobbed loudly. Shouted orders failed to quieten her, and there was a loud, ugly cracking sound as she was felled.

The rest were dragged backwards, shielding the Russians. From somewhere among the group, an AK47 spat a long burst. High at first, the last shots found marks among the still moving files of traffic.

Collisions occured as cars went out of control, their drivers hit, or gripped by blind panic. Within seconds the road was jammed, and doors were being thrown open as passengers bolted for the far side of the road.

"You reckon that's all of them?" Hyde watched the ill-assorted group making its erratic progress across the broken ground towards the chemical plant.

"I've been trying to do a head count." Revell was waiting until the range opened further before attempting pursuit. Leaving the cover of the stalled vehicles would be a dangerous move. They would have no human wall for cover. "Taking an average of three attempts, I make it twelve. Looks like we've got the lot of them."

But not yet they hadn't. Already, even hampered by their hostages, the Spetsnaz were halfway to the complex's perimeter fence.

"Once they get in there, it's going to be a hell of a job to find them." Hyde checked the spare magazine he carried. "The place must cover a whole square kilometer. It's vast."

"I can't say I'm wildy enthusiastic about conducting a fire-

179

fight in there." For the first time since they'd engaged the Russians in Munich, Revell was glad their ammunition did not include tracer rounds. Even so, a spray of any type of bullets among the pressure and storage tanks was likely to have a spectacular and lethal effect.

When four hundred meters separated them, Revell gave the order to advance. Despite the fact that it was flat, walking was not easy. Ripples of ballast and splintered ties lay hidden among the weeds.

Revell saw a woman's shoe and, within a few paces, speckles of blood on a bed of sharp granite chippings. The footwear's recent owner would be likely to slow the Russians. There was nothing Revell could do to prevent what he knew to be inevitable. A moment later there came a single shot.

Halted by the chain link fence and its topping strands of razor wire, the Russians formed the terrified civilians into a crescent about them as they tackled the obstacle.

Several shots were aimed at the advancing troops, and at three hundred meters, Revell ordered them down. Even at that distance, he could hear the wires snapping and whipping as their tension was released.

It was all a question of timing. Having almost achieved their objective, the Russians were unlikely to waste ammunition gunning down the civilians. If Revell and his men advanced too soon though, several of them would fall in the inevitable firefight.

Once through the fence, Revell was sure the Spetsnaz would abandon their hostages. They had only a strip of gravel and a perimeter road to cross, then they would be in among the mass of pipes and distillation towers that filled the site.

In that great metal maze, they could go off in any direction. So large an installation would have a substantial staff. Their presence offered fresh captives if required, and certainly replacement transport.

A burst of fire zipped overhead. Revell knew the moment had come.

"On your feet. Let's go."

If the Russians had left even one rearguard, they were an easy target now. Revell passed the sprawled body of a woman. Ahead the remainder of the civilians huddled together. Beyond them he could see the Russians sprinting for the cover of a stack of pipe fittings.

Andrea had moved out to the flank and stopped to loose off a ten-round burst. A single figure pitched forward, then recovered and tried to regain its feet.

Before Andrea could fire again, one of his comrades turned and aimed his weapon at the wounded man. He appeared to fire, but nothing happened. He threw down the pistol and went after the others.

At the last possible moment, the civilians scattered from the hole in the fence. Hyde dived through first and managed to get off a couple of aimed shots before the Russians were hidden from sight. His second found a mark. A man fell heavily. This time no one came back to try to finish him off.

The Spetsnaz in the road raised himself on one knee.

The discarded handgun was close by. Ripper took no chance. His snap shot tore into the man's throat and he toppled.

The victim of Hyde's shooting was dead, killed by a bullet that had deformed on impact against the base of his spine. It had gone on through his body to tear a huge exit wound below his ribs.

A little distance away, drops of bloods and scraps of flesh and camouflage material indicated that the sergeant's first shot had also found a mark.

"Ten left." Revell looked up, and then off to either side. In all directions the huge complex dwarfed them. "Where the do we start looking."

"They'll try to put in a bit of distance at first." Hyde picked up the pistol. "So I reckon it'll be a straight line for the first few minutes. Then they'll make a break to lose us, but whether they'll dive to the right or left . . ." He withdrew the pistol's magazine. I thought maybe that Red didn't finish off his buddy because his gun jammed. It wasn't that. It was empty."

"We can't count on them all being out of ammunition." Revell was thinking the same way as the NCO. It had to be unlikely that the Reds would set an ambush for them, but he had no delusions about the dangers of continuing the chase.

It would take only one bullet, or a grenade, to unleash all the horrors contained in the pipes and tanks about them. And besides, he and his men had already done all that could be expected of them. Hell, they weren't even supposed to be armed.

The civilians had been released, and the Spetsnaz still on the loose posed a small threat to anybody now. It could only be a matter of time before they were located and rounded up, or finished off.

From the flyover, the police would have had a grandstand view of what happened. Reinforcements were certain to be on the way. There was just no need for the him and the section to put themselves further at risk.

Even as he reasoned that way, he sensed that the others were looking at him, waiting for his decision. The same thoughts would be in their minds. Revell could be pretty certain that all of them were coming to the same conclusion.

"Okay, we're going in after them. Stay in contact, but don't bunch. No firing without a clear target. Our ammo situation isn't that much better than theirs."

They started forward, walking into the complex under a gantry that carried runs of piping over a service road. Walkways crossed and recrossed overhead. Steam hissed from of large retorts. Lights on control panels glowed an eerie green and angry red through the clouds of drifting vapor.

"Shit." Ripper looked at Andrea. "This is like walking into hell."

CHAPTER THIRTY-FIVE

A smear of blood gave them the vital information they needed. It told them the point at which the hurrying Russians had turned off the road, into the heart of the chemical plant.

Hands that must have been clutching a gaping wound, had for a moment sought support on a stanchion. In making an effort to get going again, the wounded Russian must have pushed himself off. Where his fingers had dragged and left parallel lines of blood, they pointed to the fresh heading as clearly as any signpost.

Revell and his people were in a narrow passageway this time, hemmed in by masses of complicated pipe runs. Girder latticework carried more of the same above them.

The traces of blood became more frequent. It was clear from the signs that the disabled man was having to stop and rest more frequently, was having trouble keeping up. Just as obvious was the fact that no one was offering him assistance.

Twice more the trail of blood indicated changes of direction, until they were travelling along between rows of tall anonymous distillation vessels.

With the sky overcast, it was impossible for Revell to be quite certain, but he had the feeling they had begun to go in a wide circle.

He couldn't believe that the Russians were doing it deliberately. They must have seen the police on the flyover, must know the autobahn no longer offered an escape route. So if they were going back on their tracks — and he was becoming certain they were — then they were doing it through disorientation.

Perhaps it had been brought on by exhaustion, or an accumulation of stress. Whichever it was, advantage could be taken of it, if they acted fast.

Through a gap in between the towers, Revell saw an elevated walkway. He pointed it out to Sgt. Hyde. "If we use that, I think we can get ahead of them."

Without waiting to see if he was followed, Revell started up an access ladder. Pipes that he brushed past felt warm. Some throbbed with the pulsing volumes of gas and liquid being pumped through them.

Their feet made the mesh of the catwalk rattle and clatter. The major could only hope that the other noises created by the plant would cover it. They'd travelled two hundred meters when they recognized below them a junction they had passed earlier.

Spreading out, they sought what concealment there was. Revell took up position behind an intersection of two huge pipes. His elevated vantage point gave him a clear view of the junction and the first few meters of the roads that ran into it. He didn't have to wait long.

There was no opportunity to count them. One second the road below was empty, the next the Spetsnaz were walking into their sights.

Shorts bursts and single shots lashed into the group. Suddenly and unexpectedly, those Russians who were not down were throwing away their weapons and putting their hands in the air.

Dropping down to the ground, Revell's first move was to toe away those rifles that might still be within reach. Joined by his section, Revell examined the Spetsnaz who had been hit.

Three were already dead, another three would be shortly. A mortally wounded NCO died even as Revell turned him over to remove his knife and pistol. The other two had only moments left.

Shot from above, the bullets had entered through their shoulders and upper torsos. Tearing down through their bodies, the tumbling rounds, misshapen after hitting bones, would have inflicted massive multiple injuries internally.

The three who had surrendered had escaped serious injuries, collecting no more than four flesh wounds among them. All looked as shocked as if they'd been hit badly.

"They're an ugly-looking crew." Scully appropriated a particularly nice knife as a trophy.

"Have you looked at yourself recently?" Andrea finished a tally of the captured weapons and ammunition. "Only sixteen rounds between them."

Dooley took the Soviet rifles and, resting them one at a time against a pile of cast-iron flanges, stamped them to scrap. "Has anybody noticed there's only nine of the fuckers?"

It took only a quick check to reveal that none of the dead or dying had a wound consistent with the type Sgt. Hyde had inflicted earlier.

Aware how poor his Russian was, Revell still tried to interrogate their prisoners. Though the gist of his questioning must have been understood, none made a reply. Among them at least one probably comprehended English, but nothing brought any response.

"I don't think it's that they don't understand." Revell gave up. "I think it's more that they can't be bothered."

Certainly the appearance of the captured men bore that out. Whatever training and abilities had enabled them to survive so long, it all seemed to have deserted them. With their heads hanging, their manner completely apathetic, they were like cattle waiting for slaughter. But the comparison was not that accurate. Cattle, with an awareness of death, would have become restless, fretful. These men were completely bereft of animation. If they comprehended their situation, then apparently it didn't move them at all.

Even when another of the wounded died noisily, they did not look up. When ordered, by gestures, to sit with their hands clasped on top of their heads, they did so without bothering to move themselves by so much as a single step from the

185

bodies.

"Hold them here. I'll take Andrea and backtrack. He can't be faraway. They probably bumped him off when he couldn't keep up any longer. No wonder they stand there looking like they're resigned to death. They kill their own so easily, life can't mean much to them."

Revell retraced the route by which the Spetsnaz had reached the ambush. A minute's walk brought them within sight of the missing man.

He'd expected to find a body, but even from a distance it was obvious that he was still, just, alive. The Russian was sat propped between two squat pressure tanks. The whole of his jacket was saturated in blood, and his left arm hung limp at his side. He hadn't seen them.

With his good hand, he held a small object to his mouth, and was tugging at it weakly with his teeth.

Andrea and the major fired at the same instant. Their target's body jerked under the impact, and his bloodstained hand released its grip on the grenade.

For a long moment, the dead man's jaws stayed locked on the pin, as the fragmentation bomb dangled from his mouth. Then a last rattle of breath passed his lips, and the device fell harmlessly into his lap.

Cautiously they approached the body. As they drew close, Revell noticed a thick cloud of heavy vapor was beginning to swirl about the corpse. Where it had slumped sideways, it revealed a dent and hairline fracture in one of the pressurized containers.

There was a low whistling sound as the gas escaped, and a subdued rumbling from within. A gauge attached to its side was registering wildly varying readings, as an indicator swung back and forth across the calibrations on its dial.

Whatever the composition of the leaking substance, Revell recognized its corrosive properties. Already the Russian's body was being eaten up, and the material of his battledress was smouldering. As he watched, Revell saw the vapor flow over the legs of the corpse and into its lap. The grenade began to smoke.

A moment later, with Andrea matching him pace for pace, they were running for their lives.

CHAPTER THIRTY-SIX

Revell was shouting as he ran. Perhaps he wouldn't make it, but the others had a head start, if they heeded his warning. Behind them there was a sudden thudding sound that was the charge inside the grenade detonating.

Still making a speed that threatened to burst his lungs, Revell dared hope that there would be no chain reaction. His optimism was ill-founded and short-lived.

A short sharp screech of escaping gas was abruptly smothered by a powerful explosion. It was as if a magnesium flare had been ignited. Although it was mid-afternoon, the natural light was replaced with one so vivid that the world became like a photographic negative. A surface was either in bright light or pitch-black shadow.

Feeling the heat on his back, Revell found an extra reserve of strength he'd never known he had. Even as he discovered it though, he realized that Andrea was falling behind. He reduced his speed to match hers. For an instant their eyes met, and he knew that they were going to survive or die together.

Lungs burning, they reached the junction, hurdling over five bodies as they made for the open. Now there were more explosions behind them, each louder than the one before. Blast waves were tearing through the complex, creating further damage in advance of the building fires.

Revell's foot caught a projecting piece of angle iron and he stumbled. He felt himself being grabbed by Andrea and managed to stay on his feet.

Waves of roasting heat against their backs kept them going when their bodies had no reserves left. The chemical plant was blasting itself apart, tearing its own heart out in an increasingly violent sequence of explosions.

Ahead was the perimeter road and the fence. Revell could see Dooley and Ripper struggling to pull a limp form through the rent in the wire.

A colossal blast wave smashed everyone down. Looking back, Revell saw a huge ball of crimson flame soaring to a tremendous height. At its base the great steel tanks and towers were buckling and collapsing in the heat. The torn metal of broken pipes was dripping gobs of molten steel, as fierce blowtorches of flame spouted from them.

"Leave him, he's dead." Revell flinched as red-hot bolts and plates rained down close by. "Save yourselves."

The dying Russian had been unable to withstand the attempts to manhandle him through the fence. They abandoned his body draped halfway through the opening. A moment after they left it, a huge chunk of flaming debris crushed his remains and twenty meters of fence, enveloping the area in a furnace of searing fire.

Wave after wave of gigantic explosions ripped through the complex. Huge storage tanks were blasted skywards as their contents ignited. They would rise several hundred feet, and then their thousand-ton fabric would turn on its side and fall back. The impact of the landing would send a shock through the ground that made it bounce and ripple, but the thunderous report that accompanied it was lost among the nonstop roar of fresh explosions.

From end to end, the chemical plant became a single monstrous blazing scene of destruction. Single blasts or eruptions no longer showed amongst the holocaust, a curtain of fire engulfed the site.

The autobahn was lined with the people who had returned to their vehicles. They watched the spectacle, forgetting their recent fear and the reason for their panicking flight.

Under their feet lay the corpse of the old man. It was totally ignored, except when it was cursed by someone tripping over it, or when they were forced to step across it to get to a better vantage point.

Andrea, Revell, and the rest of section were also watching, as they sat exhausted, still recovering from the race for their lives. They looked up as a pair of Blackhawk helicopters circled low, then came in for a fast landing nearby.

Squads of heavily armed men were jumping from each before the wheels touched, immediately forming a protective perimeter until the choppers lifted again.

A figure strode confidently and purposefully towards the resting group. Revell recognized the SAS colonel. He was flanked by two heavily armed troopers.

"Did you account for them all?"

Revell didn't bother to stand. "Most of them."

"What the hell do you mean by that? What's the body count?"

Sighing, Revell pushed himself to his feet. He felt old and tired. "Between our own efforts and theirs, we accounted for nine of them altogether. All confirmed. The bodies are back in there." He indicated the kilometer-long pyre. Even at that distance the heat could still be felt.

"The others got away? You missed them?"

With the palm of his hands, the colonel was impatiently slapping the twin holsters he sported.

"No, we got them, then they must have made a break for it when the plant went up. It was every man for himself in there. Maybe they struck out the wrong way. Who knows?"

"What sort of body count is that? First you let them go, then you don't know which way they went, now you aren't even sure if they made it or not!"

"Colonel, I don't give a fuck about your body count."

The trooper-bodyguards stepped forward aggressively, and found themselves instantly confronting Revell's men. Weapons were levelled, Andrea gripping the pin of a grenade.

190

"Bloody private armies." The colonel waved forward the rest of his men. "Even got a bloody woman. Still, I expect she comes in useful."

The colonel had been looking at Andrea. He certainly never saw Revell's fist. Connecting with the side of his face, the blow rocked him, but he stayed on his feet.

"That you'll regret."

"I wouldn't be too hasty, Colonel." Revell indicated the road. Above the roofs of the cars, on the south-bound carriageway, were visible the newly arrived transport of the remainder of the Special Combat Company.

Debussing, the men swarmed through the traffic to make the odds more than even.

Forcing himself to stay calm and remain outwardly under control, the colonel seethed inside. He sensed the dangerous mood of his men, after the insult of the blow.

"So what do you intend doing now, with this ragbag outfit of freaks and misfits?"

"We're neither of those things, Colonel."

Revell knew without looking that his virtually unarmed company was backing him up.

"Since the Zone took shape, we've been in there getting results, doing ten times more damage than your pinprick raids."

"That's it, Major." Dooley cheered. "Give it to the cunt, good and strong."

"Then why don't you get back in there?"

The colonel would have liked to launch his men against this rabble, but was acutely aware of the thousand strong civilian audience on the autobahn, now joined by a large number of West German police.

"That's just where we're going." Revell ripped off his NATO insignia. "This time though we'll be fighting for ourselves."

"Going freelance, are you?" The colonel sneered. "That's about all you're fit for, but you'll never make it. I'll see to that."

Revell took the grenade from Andrea, and pulled out the

pin. "You're going to help us make it. Unless you reckon you can outrun a grenade, have your men hand over their weapons and ammunition."

It was a long moment before the colonel spoke. When he ordered his men to comply, it was with a hoarse, emotion-choked voice. He had to repeat himself several times before all of them reluctantly obeyed.

"We'll be on our way then. Thanks for the equipment." Revell tossed the grenade into a culvert, where it exploded harmlessly, but started a short-lived panic among the civilian watchers.

"You'll never get there."

"Yes, we will, Colonel. No one is going to stop us. We've a war to fight, and we've only just started."